"How have you been?" he asked.

Pregnant.

The word was on the tip of Kayla's tongue because, of course, that reality had been at the forefront of her mind since the little plus sign had appeared on the test she'd bought at the pharmacy in Kalispell. But she didn't dare say it aloud, because she knew he couldn't understand when he didn't even remember sleeping with her.

"Fine," she said instead. "And you?"

"Fine," he echoed.

She nodded.

An awkward silence followed.

"I wanted to call you," he said, dropping his voice to ensure that his words wouldn't be overheard by any passersby. "There were so many times I thought about picking up the phone, just because I was thinking about you."

Her heart, already racing, accelerated even more. "You were thinking about me?"

"I haven't stopped thinking about you since we danced at the wedding."

Since we danced?

That was what Trey remembered about that night? She didn't know whether to laugh or cry.

* * *

MONTANA MAVERICKS:
What Happened at the Wedding?
A weekend Rust Creek Falls will never forget!

Dear Reader,

Five months after the event, residents of Rust Creek Falls are still talking about "what happened at the wedding"—and wondering who spiked the punch! Thankfully no one seems to know anything about what happened between Kayla Dalton and Trey Strickland that night, but it's a secret the expectant parents won't be able to keep forever...

Writing *Merry Christmas, Baby Maverick!* brought back many happy memories of the holiday before my first son was born. Although it was a lot of years ago, a mother never forgets the joyful—and frequently fearful—anticipation of welcoming a child. And through all the usual excitement of that festive season, I was already looking forward to the next, when my baby would be squirming in my arms instead of in my (hugely pregnant) belly...

What are some of your favorite holiday memories? Share them with me on Facebook or Twitter (@BrendaHarlen) or drop me a line through my website, brendaharlen.com.

Happy holidays!

Brenda Harlen

Merry Christmas, Baby Maverick!

Brenda Harlen

HARLEQUIN® SPECIAL EDITION®

Special thanks and acknowledgment to Brenda Harlen
for her contribution to the
Montana Mavericks: What Happened at the Wedding? continuity.

ISBN-13: 978-0-373-65927-2

Merry Christmas, Baby Maverick!

Copyright © 2015 by Harlequin Books S.A.

Recycling programs for this product may not exist in your area.

Printed in U.S.A.

www.Harlequin.com

Brenda Harlen is a former attorney who once had the privilege of appearing before the Supreme Court of Canada. The practice of law taught her a lot about the world and reinforced her determination to become a writer—because in fiction, she could promise a happy ending! Now she is an award-winning, national bestselling author of more than thirty titles for Harlequin. You can keep up-to-date with Brenda on Facebook and Twitter or through her website, brendaharlen.com.

Books by Brenda Harlen

Harlequin Special Edition

Those Engaging Garretts!

The Bachelor Takes a Bride
A Forever Kind of Family
The Daddy Wish
A Wife for One Year
The Single Dad's Second Chance
A Very Special Delivery
His Long-Lost Family
From Neighbors...to Newlyweds?

Montana Mavericks: 20 Years in the Saddle!

The Maverick's Thanksgiving Baby

Montana Mavericks: Rust Creek Cowboys

A Maverick under the Mistletoe

Montana Mavericks: Back in the Saddle

The Maverick's Ready-Made Family

Reigning Men

Royal Holiday Bride
Prince Daddy & the Nanny

Visit the Author Profile page at Harlequin.com for more titles.

For loyal readers of all the Montana Mavericks series, from Whitehorn to Thunder Canyon and Rust Creek Falls.

This book is also dedicated to Robin Harlen (May 8, 1943–December 20, 2014)— a wonderful father-in-law to me and granddad to my children. He would be pleased to know that I finished this book on schedule.

Prologue

Fourth of July

Trey Strickland did a double take when he first spotted Kayla Dalton at the wedding of local rancher Braden Traub to Jennifer MacCallum of Whitehorn.

Although Trey was only visiting from Thunder Canyon, his family had lived in Rust Creek Falls for a number of years while he was growing up. His best friend during that time was Derek Dalton, who had two older brothers, Eli and Jonah, and two younger sisters, twins Kristen and Kayla.

Trey remembered Kayla as a pretty girl with a quiet demeanor and a shy smile, but she'd grown up—and then some. She was no longer a pretty girl, but a beautiful woman with long, silky brown hair, sparkling blue eyes and distinctly feminine curves. Looking at her now, he couldn't help but notice the lean, shapely legs showcased by the short hem of her blue sundress, the tiny waist encircled by a narrow belt, the sweetly rounded breasts hugged by the bodice…and his mouth actually went dry.

She was stunning, sexy and incredibly tempting. Unfortunately, she was still his friend's little sister, which meant that she was off-limits to him.

But apparently, Kayla was unaware of that fact, because after hovering on the other side of the wooden dance floor that had been erected in the park for the occasion, she set down her cup of punch and made her way around the perimeter of the crowd.

She had a purposeful stride—and surprisingly long legs for such a little thing—and he enjoyed watching her move. He was pleased when she came to a stop beside him, looking up at him with determination and just a little bit of trepidation glinting in her beautiful blue eyes.

"Hello, Trey."

He inclined his head in acknowledgment of her greeting. "Kayla."

For some reason, his use of her name seemed to take her aback. "How did you know it was me?"

"I haven't been gone from Rust Creek Falls *that* long," he chided gently.

Soft pink color filled her cheeks. "I meant—how did you know I was Kayla and not Kristen?"

"I'm not sure," he admitted. But the truth was, he'd never had any trouble telling his friend's twin sisters apart. Although identical in appearance, their personalities were completely different, and he'd always had a soft spot for the shyer twin.

Thankfully, she didn't press for more of an explanation, turning her attention back to the dance floor instead. "They look good together, don't they?"

He followed her gaze to the bride and groom, nodded.

They chatted a little bit more about the wedding and

various other things. A couple of older women circulated through the crowd, carrying cups of wedding punch to distribute to the guests. The beverage was refreshingly cold, so he lifted a couple of cups from the tray and handed one to Kayla.

When they finished their drinks and set the empty cups aside, he turned to her and asked, "Would you like to dance?"

She seemed surprised by the question and hesitated for a moment before nodding. "Yes, I would."

Of course, that was the moment the tempo of the music changed from a quick, boot-stomping tune to a soft, seductive melody. Then Kayla stepped into his arms, and the intoxicating effect of her soft curves against him shot through his veins like the most potent whiskey.

A strand of her hair had come loose from the fancy twist at the back of her head and it fluttered in the breeze, tickling his throat. The scent of her skin teased his nostrils, stirring his blood and clouding his brain. He tried to think logically about the situation—just because she was an attractive woman and he was attracted didn't mean he had to act on the feeling. But damn, it was hard to remember all the reasons why he needed to resist when she fit so perfectly against him.

As the song began to wind down, he guided her to the edge of the dance floor, then through the crowd of people mingling, until they were in the shadows of the pavilion.

"I thought, for a moment, you were going to drag me all the way to your room at the boarding house," Kayla teased.

The idea was more than a little tempting. "I might have," he said. "If I thought you would let me."

She held his gaze for a long minute then nodded slowly. "I would let you."

The promise in her eyes echoed her words. Still, he

hesitated, because this was Kayla—*Derek's sister*—and she was off-limits. But she was so tempting and pretty, and with her chin tipped up, he could see the reflection of the stars in her eyes. Dazzling. Seductive. Irresistible.

He gave in to the desire churning through him and lowered his head to kiss her.

And she kissed him back.

As her lips moved beneath his, she swayed into him. The soft press of her sweet body set his own on fire. He wrapped his arms around her, pulling her closer as he deepened the kiss. She met the searching thrust of his tongue with her own, not just responding to his demands but making her own. Apparently, sweet, shy Kayla Dalton wasn't as sweet and shy as he'd always believed—a stunning realization that further fanned the flames of his desire.

He wanted her—desperately and immediately. And the way she was molded to him, he would bet the ranch that she wanted him, too. A suspicion that was further confirmed when he started to ease his mouth away and she whimpered a soft protest, pressing closer.

"Maybe we should continue this somewhere a little more private," he suggested.

"More private sounds good," she agreed without hesitation.

He took her hand, linking their fingers together, and led her away.

Chapter One

Kayla walked out of the specialty bath shop with another bag to add to the half dozen she already carried and a feeling of satisfaction. It was only the first of December, and she was almost finished with her Christmas shopping. She'd definitely earned a hot chocolate.

Making her way toward the center court of the mall, she passed a long line of children and toddlers impatiently tugging on the hands of parents and grandparents, along with babies sleeping in carriers or snuggled in loving arms. At the end of the line was their destination: Santa.

She paused to watch as a new mom and dad approached the jolly man in the red suit, sitting on opposite sides of him after gently setting their sleeping baby girl—probably not more than a few months old—in his arms. Then the baby opened her eyes, took one look at the stranger and let out an earsplitting scream of disapproval.

While the parents fussed, trying to calm their infant daughter so the impatient photographer could snap a "First

Christmas with Santa" picture, Kayla was suddenly struck by the realization that she might be doing the same thing next Christmas.

Except that there wouldn't be a daddy in her picture, an extra set of hands to help console their unhappy baby. Kayla was on her own. Unmarried. Alone. A soon-to-be single mother who was absolutely terrified about that fact.

She'd always been logical and levelheaded, not the type of woman who acted impulsively or recklessly. Not until the Fourth of July, when she'd accepted Trey's invitation to go back to his room. One cup of wedding punch had helped rekindle her schoolgirl fantasies about the man who had been her brother's best friend. Then one dance had led to one kiss—and one impulsive decision to one unplanned pregnancy.

She owed it to Trey to tell him that their night together had resulted in a baby, but she didn't know how to break the news when he apparently didn't even remember that they'd been together. Even now, five months later, that humiliation made her cheeks burn.

She wasn't at all promiscuous. In fact, Trey was the first man she'd had sex with in three years and only the second in all of her twenty-five years. But Trey had also been drinking the wedding punch that was later rumored to have been spiked with something, and his memory of events after they got back to his room at the boarding house was a little hazy. Kayla had been relieved—and just a little insulted—when he left Rust Creek Falls to return to Thunder Canyon a few weeks later without another word to her about what had happened between them.

But she knew that he would be back again. Trey no longer lived in Rust Creek Falls but his grandparents—Gene and Melba Strickland—still did, and he returned two or three times every year to visit them. It was inevitable that their paths would cross when he came back, and she'd have to tell him about their baby when he did.

Until then, she was grateful that she'd managed to keep her pregnancy a secret from almost everyone else. Even now, only her sister, Kristen, knew the truth. Thankfully, she'd only just started to show, and the cold Montana weather gave her the perfect excuse to don big flannel shirts or bulky sweaters that easily covered the slight curve of her belly.

Regardless of the circumstances of conception, she was happy about the baby and excited about impending motherhood. It was only the "single" part that scared her. And although her family would likely disapprove of the situation, she was confident they would ultimately support her and love her child as much as she did.

The tiny life stirred inside her, making her smile. She loved her baby so much already, so much more than she would have imagined possible, but she had no illusions that Trey would be as happy about the situation. Especially considering that he didn't even remember getting naked and tangling up the sheets with her.

She pushed those worries aside for another day and entered the line in the café. After perusing the menu for several minutes, she decided on a peppermint hot chocolate with extra whipped cream, chocolate drizzle and candy-cane sprinkles. She'd been careful not to overindulge, conscious of having to disguise every pound she put on, but she couldn't hide her pregnancy forever—probably not even for much longer.

Which, of course, introduced another dilemma—how could she tell anyone else about the baby when she hadn't even told the baby's father? And what if he denied that it was his?

The sweet beverage she'd sipped suddenly left a bad taste in her mouth as she considered the possibility.

A denial from Trey would devastate her, but she knew that she had to be prepared for it. If he didn't remember sleeping with her, why would he believe he was the father of her child?

"It really is a small world, isn't it?"

Kayla started at the question that interrupted her thoughts, her face flaming as she glanced up to see Trey's grandmother standing beside her table with a steaming cup of coffee in her hands. Not that Melba Strickland could possibly know what she'd been thinking, but Kayla couldn't help but feel unnerved by the other woman's unexpected presence.

She forced a smile. "Yes, it is," she agreed.

"Do you mind if I join you?"

"Of course not." There weren't many empty chairs in the café, and it seemed silly for each of them to sit alone as if they were strangers. Especially considering that Kayla had known the Stricklands for as long as she could remember.

Melba and Gene were good people, if a little old-fashioned. Or maybe it was just that they were old—probably in their late seventies or early eighties, she guessed, because no one seemed to know for sure. Regardless, their boarding house was a popular place for people looking for long-term accommodations in Rust Creek Falls—so long as they didn't mind abiding by Melba's strict rules, which included a ban on overnight visitors. An explicit prohibition that Kayla and Trey had ignored on the Fourth of July.

"Goodness, this place is bustling." Melba pulled back the empty chair and settled into it. "The whole mall, I mean. It's only the first of December, and the stores are packed. It's as if everyone in Kalispell has decided to go shopping today."

"Everyone in Kalispell and half of Rust Creek Falls," Kayla agreed.

The older woman chuckled. "Looks like you got an early start," she noted, glancing at the shopping bags beneath the table.

"Very early," Kayla agreed, scooping up some whipped cream and licking it off the spoon.

"I love everything about Christmas," Melba confided. "The shopping and wrapping, decorating and baking. But mostly I love the time we spend with family and friends."

"Are you going to have a full house over the holidays this year?" Kayla asked.

"I hope so," the older woman said. "We've had Claire, Levi and Bekka with us since August, and Claire's sisters have hinted that they might head this way for Christmas, which would be great. I so love having the kids around."

Kayla smiled because she knew the *kids* referred to— Bekka excluded—were all adults.

They chatted some more about holiday traditions and family plans, then Melba glanced at the clock on the wall. "Goodness—" her eyes grew wide "—is that the time? I've only got three hours until I'm meeting Gene for dinner, and all I've bought is a cup of coffee."

"Mr. Strickland came into the city with you?"

The older woman nodded. "We've got tickets to see *A Christmas Carol* tonight."

"I'm sure you'll enjoy it," Kayla said. "The whole cast— especially Belle—is fabulous."

Melba smiled at her mention of the character played on the stage by Kayla's sister. "Not that you're biased at all," she said with a wink.

"Well, maybe a little." Her sister had always loved the

theater, but she'd been away from it for a lot of years before deciding to audition for the holiday production in Kalispell. The part of Scrooge's former fiancée wasn't a major role, but it was an opportunity for Kristen to get back on stage, and she was loving every minute of it.

In support of her sister, Kayla had signed on to help behind the scenes. She'd been surprised to discover how much she enjoyed the work—and grateful that keeping busy allowed her to pretend her whole life wasn't about to change.

"Lissa and Gage saw it last week and said the costumes were spectacular."

"I had fun working on them," she acknowledged.

"But you have no desire to wear them onstage?"

"None at all."

"You know, Kristen's ease at playing different roles has some people wondering if she might be the Rust Creek Rambler."

Kayla frowned. "You're kidding."

"Of course, I wouldn't expect you to betray your sister if she is the author of the gossip column."

"She's not," Kayla said firmly.

"I'm sure you would know—they say twins have no secrets from one another," Melba said. "Besides, she's been so busy with the play—and now with her new fiancé—when would she have time to write it?"

"I'm a little surprised there's been so much recent interest in uncovering the identity of the anonymous author, when the column has been around for almost three years now."

"Three and a half," Melba corrected, proving Kayla's point. "I suspect interest has piqued because some people think the Rambler is responsible for spiking the punch at the wedding."

Kayla gasped. "Why would they think that?"

"The events of that night have certainly provided a lot of fodder for the column over the past few months," the older woman pointed out. "It almost makes sense that whoever is writing it might want to help generate some juicy stories."

"That's a scary thought."

"Isn't it?" Melba finished her coffee and set her cup down. "The Rambler also noted that you were up close and personal with my grandson, Trey, on the dance floor at Braden and Jennifer's wedding."

Kayla had long ago accepted that in order to ensure no one ever suspected she was the Rambler, it was necessary to drop her own name into the column every once in a while. Since her turn on the dance floor with Trey hadn't gone unnoticed, the Rambler would be expected to comment on it. As for *up close and personal*—that hadn't come until later, and she had no intention of confiding *that* truth to Trey's grandmother.

Instead, she lifted her cup to her lips—only to discover that it was empty. She set it down again. "We danced," she admitted.

"That's all?" Melba sounded almost disappointed.

"That's all," Kayla echoed, her cheeks flushing. She'd never been a very good liar, and lying to Trey's grandmother—her own baby's great-grandmother—wasn't easy, even if it was necessary.

The older woman sighed. "I've been hoping for a long time that Trey would find a special someone to settle down with. If I had my choice, that special someone would live in Rust Creek Falls, so that he'd want to come back home here—or at least visit more often."

"Maybe he already has someone special in Thunder Canyon," she suggested, aiming for a casual tone.

"I'm sure he would have told me if he did," Melba said. "I know he sees girls, but he's never been serious about any of them. No one except Lana."

"Lana?" she echoed.

Melba's brow furrowed. "Maybe you don't know about Lana. I guess Jerry and Barbara had already moved away from Rust Creek Falls before Trey met her."

Kayla hadn't considered that the father of her baby might be involved with someone else—or that he might even have been in a relationship when he was visiting in the summer. Thinking about the possibility now made her feel sick. She honestly didn't think Trey was that kind of guy—but the reality was that neither of them had been thinking very clearly the night of the wedding.

"Anyway, he met Lana at some small local rodeo, where she won the division championship for barrel racing," the other woman continued. "I think it was actually her horse that caught his eye before she did, but it wasn't too long after that they were inseparable.

"They were together for almost two years, and apparently Trey had even started looking at engagement rings. And then—" Melba shook her head "—Lana was out on her horse, just enjoying a leisurely trail ride, when the animal got spooked by something and threw her."

Kayla winced, already anticipating how the story would end.

"She sustained some pretty serious injuries, and died five days later. She was only twenty-three years old."

"Trey must have been devastated," Kayla said softly, her heart aching for his loss.

"He was," Melba agreed. "We were all saddened by her death—and so worried about him. But then, when I heard that he was dancing with you at the wedding, well,

I have to admit, I let myself hope it was a sign that his heart was healed."

"It was just a dance," she said again.

"Maybe it was," Melba acknowledged, as she pushed her chair away from the table. "And maybe there will be something more when you see him again."

"Did you leave any presents in the mall for anyone else to buy?" Kristen teased, as she helped her sister cart her parcels and packages into the sprawling log house they'd grown up in.

The Circle D Ranch, located on the north side of town, was still home to Kayla, but her twin had moved out a few weeks earlier, into a century-old Victorian home that their brother Jonah had bought after the flood for the purposes of rehabbing and reselling. Since Kristen had started working at the theater in Kalispell, this house, on the south edge of town and close to the highway, had significantly cut down her commuting time—and given her a taste of the independence she'd been craving.

"Only a few," Kayla warned her, dumping her armload of packages onto her bed.

"That one looks interesting," her sister said, reaching for the bag from the bath shop.

Kayla slapped her hand away. "No snooping."

"Then it *is* for me," Kristen deduced.

"You'll find out at Christmas—unless you try to peek again, in which case it's going back to the store."

"I won't peek," her sister promised. "But speaking of shopping, I was thinking that you should plan a trip to Thunder Canyon to check out the stores there."

Kayla gestured to the assortment of bags. "Does it look like I need to check out any more stores?"

Kristen rolled her eyes. "You and I know that your

shopping is done—or very nearly, but no one else needs to know that. And shopping is only a cover story, anyway—your *real* purpose would be to see Trey and *finally* tell him about the secret you've been keeping for far too long."

Just the idea of seeing Trey again made Kayla's tummy tighten in knots of apprehension and her heart pound with anticipation. Thoughts of Trey had always had that effect on her; his actual presence was even more potent.

She *really* liked him—in fact, she'd had a major crush on him for a lot of years when she was younger. Then his family had moved away, and her infatuated heart had moved on. Until the next time he came back to Rust Creek Falls, and all it would take was a smile or a wave and she would be swooning again.

But still, her infatuation had been nothing more than a harmless fantasy—until the night of the wedding. Being with Trey had stirred all those old feelings up again and even now there was, admittedly, a part of her that hoped he'd be thrilled by the news of a baby, sweep her into his arms, declare that he'd always loved her and wanted to marry her so they could raise their child together.

Unfortunately, the reality was that five months had passed since the night they'd spent together, and she hadn't heard a single word from him after he'd gone back to Thunder Canyon.

She'd been pathetically smitten and easily seduced, and he'd been so drunk he didn't even remember being with her. Of course, another and even more damning possibility was that he *did* remember but was only pretending not to because he was ashamed by what had happened—a possibility that did not bode well for the conversation they needed to have.

"I know I have to talk to Trey," she acknowledged to

her sister now. "But I can't just show up in Thunder Canyon to tell him that I'm having his baby."

"Why not?" Kristen demanded.

"Because."

"You've been making excuses for months," her sister pointed out. "And you don't have many more left—excuses *or* months."

"Do you think I don't realize that?"

Kristen threw her hands up. "I don't know what you realize. I never thought you'd keep your pregnancy a secret for so long—not from me or the rest of your family, and especially not from the baby's father.

"I've tried to be understanding and supportive," her sister continued. "But if you don't tell him, *I* will."

Kayla knew it wasn't an idle threat. "But how can I tell Trey that he's going to be a father when he doesn't even remember having sex with me?"

Kristen frowned. "What are you talking about?"

"When I saw Trey—later the next day—he said that his memory of the night before was hazy."

"A lot of people had blank patches after drinking that spiked punch."

She nodded. "But Trey's mind had apparently blanked out the whole part about getting naked with me."

"Okay, that might make the conversation a little awkward," Kristen acknowledged.

"You think?"

Her sister ignored her sarcasm. "But awkward or not, you have to get it over with. I'd say sooner rather than later, but it's already later."

"I know," Kayla agreed.

"So…shopping trip to Thunder Canyon?" Kristen prompted.

"Three hundred miles is a long way to go to pick up

a few gifts—don't you think Mom and Dad will be suspicious?"

"I think Mom and Dad should be the least of your worries right now."

Kristen was right, of course. Her sister always had a way of cutting to the heart of the matter. "Will you go with me?"

"If I had two consecutive days off from the theater, I would, but it's just not possible right now."

She nodded.

"And no," Kristen spoke up before Kayla could say anything more. "That does not give you an excuse to wait until after the holidays to make the trip."

"I know," she grumbled, because she had, of course, been thinking exactly that—and her sister knew her well enough to know it.

"So when are you going?" Kristen demanded.

"I'll keep you posted. I have to get to the paper."

RUST CREEK RAMBLINGS: THE LA LAWYER TAKES A BRIDE

Yes, folks, it's official: attorney to the stars Ryan Roarke is off the market after being firmly lassoed by a local cowgirl! So what's the next order of business for the California lawyer? Filing for a change of venue in order to keep his boots firmly planted on Montana soil and close to his beautiful bride-to-be, Kristen Dalton. No details are available yet on a date for the impending nuptials, but the good people of Rust Creek Falls can rest assured that they will know as soon as the Rambler does…

Chapter Two

Trey Strickland had been happily living near and working at the Thunder Canyon Resort for several years now, but he never passed up an opportunity to visit his grandparents in Rust Creek Falls. His family had lived in the small town for nearly a decade while he was growing up, and he still had good friends there and always enjoyed catching up with them again.

Now it was December and he hadn't been back since the summer. And whenever he thought of that visit, he thought of Kayla Dalton. Truth be told, he thought of Kayla at other times, too—and that was one of the reasons he'd forced himself to stay away for so long.

He'd slept with his best friend's little sister.

And he didn't regret it.

Unfortunately, he wasn't sure he could say the same about Kayla based on her demeanor toward him the next day. She'd pretended nothing had happened between them, so he'd followed her lead.

He suspected that they'd both acted out of character as a result of being under the influence of the wedding punch. According to his grandmother, the police now believed the fruity concoction had been spiked and were trying to determine who had done so and why.

Trey's initial reaction to the news had been shock, followed quickly by relief that there was a credible explanation for his own reckless behavior that night. But whatever had been in the punch, the remnants of it had long since been purged from his system, yet thoughts and memories of Kayla continued to tease his mind.

As he navigated the familiar route from Thunder Canyon to Rust Creek Falls, his mind wandered. He was looking forward to spending the holidays with his grandparents, but he was mostly focused on the anticipation of seeing Kayla again, and the closer he got to his destination, the more prominent she figured in his thoughts.

He'd had a great time with her at the wedding. Prior to that night, they hadn't exchanged more than a few dozen words over the past several years, so he'd been surprised to discover that she was smart and witty and fun. She was the kind of woman he enjoyed spending time with, and he hoped he would get to spend more time with her when he was in town.

But first he owed her an apology, which he would have delivered the very next morning except that his brain had still been enveloped in some kind of fog that had prevented him from remembering exactly what had happened after the wedding.

He didn't usually drink to excess. Sure, he enjoyed hanging out with his buddies and having a few beers, but he'd long outgrown the desire to get drunk and suffer the consequences the next morning. But whatever had been in that wedding punch, it hadn't given any hint of its incredible potency...

It was morning.

The bright sunlight slipping past the edges of the curtains told him that much. The only other fact that registered in his brain was that he was dying. Or at least he felt as if he was. The pain in his head was so absolutely excruciating, he was certain it was going to fall right off his body—and there was a part of him that wished it would.

In a desperate attempt to numb the torturous agony, he downed a handful of aspirin with a half gallon of water then managed to sit upright without wincing.

The quiet knock on his door echoed like a thunderclap in his head before his grandmother entered. She clucked her tongue in disapproval when she came into his room and threw the curtains wide, the sunlight stabbing through his eyeballs like hot knives.

"Get up and out of bed," she told him. "It's laundry day and I need your sheets."

He pulled the covers up over his head. "My sheets are busy right now."

"You should be, too. Your grandfather could use a hand cleaning out the shed."

He tried to nod, but even that was painful. "Give me half an hour."

He showered and dressed then turned his attention to the bed because, as his grandmother was fond of reminding him, it wasn't a hotel and she wasn't his maid. So he untucked one corner and pulled them off the bed. There was a quiet clunk as something fell free of the sheet and onto the floor.

An earring?

He slowly bent down to retrieve the sparkly teardrop, his mind immediately flashing back to the night before, when he'd stood beside Kayla Dalton on the edge of the dance floor and noticed the pretty earrings that hung from her ears.

Kayla Dalton?

He curled his fingers around the delicate bauble and sank onto the edge of the mattress as other images flashed through his mind, like snapshots with no real connection to any particular time and place. He rubbed his fingers against his temples as he tried to recall what had happened, but his brain refused to cooperate. He'd danced with Kayla—he was sure he remembered dancing with her. And then...

He frowned as he struggled to put the disjointed pieces together. She'd looked so beautiful in the moonlight, and she'd smelled really good. And her lips had looked so temptingly soft. He'd wanted to kiss her, but he didn't think he would have made that kind of move. Because as beautiful and tempting as she was, she was still Derek's sister.

But when he closed his eyes, he could almost feel the yielding of her sweet mouth beneath his, the softness of her feminine curves against his body. Since he'd never had a very good imagination, he could only conclude that the kiss had really happened.

And in order for her earring to end up in his bed—well, he had to assume that Kayla had been there, too.

And what did it say about him that he didn't even remember? Of course, it was entirely possible that they'd gotten into bed together and both passed out. Not something to be particularly proud of but, under the circumstances, probably the best possible scenario.

He tucked the earring in his pocket and finished stripping the bed, shaking out the sheets and pillowcases to ensure there weren't any other hidden treasures inside. Thankfully, there were not. Then he saw the cor-

ner of something peeking out from beneath the bed—and scooped up an empty condom wrapper.

He closed his eyes and swore.

The idea that he'd slept with Kayla Dalton had barely sunk into his brain when he saw her later that day.

She'd been polite and friendly, if a little reserved, and she'd given absolutely no indication that anything had happened between them, making him doubt all of his own conclusions about the night before.

It had taken a long time for his memories of that night to come into focus, for him to remember.

And now that those memories were clear, he was determined to talk to Kayla about what happened that night—and where they would go from here.

Kayla was on her way to the newspaper office when she spotted Trey's truck parked outside the community center.

She'd heard that he was coming back to Rust Creek Falls for the holidays, but she wasn't ready to face him. Not yet. There were still three weeks until Christmas. Why was he here already? She needed more time to plan and prepare, to figure out what to say, how to share the news that she knew would turn his whole world upside down.

The back of his truck was filled with boxes and the doors to the building were open. She'd heard that last year's gift drive for the troops was being affiliated with Thunder Canyon's Presents for Patriots this year, and she suspected that the boxes were linked to that effort.

"Kayla—hi."

She didn't need to look up to know it was Trey who was speaking. It wasn't just that she'd recognized his voice, it was that her heart was racing the way it always did whenever she was near him.

But she glanced up, her gaze skimming at least six feet

from his well-worn cowboy boots to his deep green eyes, and managed a smile. "Hi, Trey."

"This is a pleasant surprise," he said, flashing an easy grin that suggested he was genuinely happy to see her.

Which didn't really make any sense. She not only hadn't seen the guy in four months, she hadn't spoken a single word to him in that time, either. There had been no exchange of emails or text messages or any communication at all. Not that she'd expected any, but her infatuated heart had dared to hope—and been sorely wounded as a result of that silly hope.

"How have you been?" he asked.

Pregnant.

The word was on the tip of her tongue because, of course, that reality had been at the forefront of her mind since she'd seen the little plus sign in the window of the test. But she didn't dare say it aloud, because she knew he couldn't understand the relevance of the information when he didn't even remember sleeping with her.

"Fine," she said instead. "And you?"

"Fine," he echoed.

She nodded.

An awkward silence followed, which they both tried to break at the same time.

"Well, I should—"

"Maybe I could—"

Then they both stopped talking again.

"What were you going to say?" Trey asked her.

"Just that I should be going—I'm on my way to the newspaper office."

"Do you work there?"

She nodded. "I'm a copy editor."

"Oh."

And that seemed to exhaust that topic of conversation.

"It was good to see you, Trey."

"You, too."

She started past him, relieved that this first and undeniably awkward encounter was over. Her heart was pounding and her stomach was a mass of knots, but she'd managed to exchange a few words with him without bursting into tears or otherwise falling to pieces. A good first step, she decided.

"Kayla—wait."

And with those two words, her opportunity to flee with her dignity intact was threatened.

Since she hadn't moved far enough away to be able to pretend that she hadn't heard him, she reluctantly turned back.

He took a step closer.

"I wanted to call you," he said, dropping his voice to ensure that his words wouldn't be overheard by any passersby. "There were so many times I thought about picking up the phone, just because I was thinking about you."

Her heart, already racing, accelerated even more. "You were thinking about me?"

"I haven't stopped thinking about you since we danced at the wedding."

Since we danced?

That was what he remembered about that night?

She didn't know whether to laugh or cry. Under other circumstances, it might have been flattering to think that a few minutes in his arms had made such a lasting impression. Under her current circumstances, the lack of any impression of what had come afterward was hurtful and humiliating.

"I really do have to go. My boss is expecting me."

"What are you doing later?"

She frowned. "Tonight?"

"Sure."

"I'm going to the movies with Natalie Crawford."

"Oh."

He sounded so sincerely disappointed, she wanted to cancel her plans and agree to anything he wanted. Except that kind of thinking was responsible for her current predicament.

"Well, I guess I'll see you around," she said.

He held her gaze for another minute before he nodded. "Count on it."

She walked away, knowing that she already did and cursing the traitorous yearning of her heart.

Trey helped finish unloading the truck, then headed over to the boarding house. He arrived just as his grandmother was slicing into an enormous roast, and the tantalizing aroma made his mouth water.

"Mmm, something smells good."

Melba set down her utensils and wiped her hands on a towel before she crossed the room to envelop him in a warm hug. "I was hoping you'd be here in time for dinner."

"I'd tell you that I ignored the speed limit to make sure of it, but my grandmother would probably disapprove," he teased.

"She certainly would," Melba agreed sternly.

"In time for dinner but not in time to mash the potatoes," Claire said, as she finished her assigned task.

His grandmother let him go and turned him over to his cousin, who hugged him tight.

He tipped her chin up to look into her brown eyes. "Everything good?"

"Everything's great," she assured him, her radiant smile confirming the words.

"Levi?" he prompted, referring to the husband she'd briefly separated from in the summer.

"In the front parlor, playing with Bekka."

"It's so much fun to have a child in the house again," their grandmother said. "I can't wait for there to be a dozen more."

"Don't count on me to add another dozen," Claire warned. "I have my hands full with one."

"At least you've given me one," Melba noted, with a pointed glance in Trey's direction.

He moved to the sink and washed his hands. "What can I do to help with dinner?" he asked, desperate to change the topic of conversation.

"You can get down the pitcher for the gravy." Melba gestured to a cupboard far over her head. "Then round up the rest of the family."

Trey retrieved the pitcher, then gratefully escaped from the kitchen. Of course, he should have expected the conversation would circle back to the topic of marriage and babies during the meal.

"So what's been going on in town since I've been gone?" he asked, scooping up a forkful of the potatoes Claire had mashed.

"Goodness, I don't know where to begin," his grandmother said. "Oh—the Santa Claus parade was last weekend and the Dalton girl got engaged."

The potatoes he'd just swallowed dropped to the bottom of his stomach like a ball of lead. "Kayla?"

His grandmother shook her head. "Her sister, Kristen."

Trey exhaled slowly.

He didn't know why he'd immediately assumed Kayla, maybe because he'd seen her so recently and had been thinking about her for so long, but the thought of her with another man—*engaged* to another man—had hit him like a physical jab.

He'd been away from Rust Creek Falls for months—it wasn't just possible but likely that Kayla had gone out with other guys during that time. And why shouldn't she? They'd spent one night together—they didn't have a relationship.

And even if they did, he wasn't looking to fall in love and get married. So why did the idea of her being with another man make him a little bit crazy?

"Who'd she get engaged to?" he asked, picking up the thread of the conversation again.

"Maggie Roarke's brother, Ryan," Claire said.

Trey didn't know Ryan Roarke, but he worked with his brother, Shane, at the Thunder Canyon Resort. And he knew that their sister had moved to Rust Creek Falls the previous year. "Maggie's the new lawyer in town—the one married to Jesse Crawford?"

His grandmother nodded. "She gave up her fancy office in LA to make a life here with Jesse, because they were in love."

"I thought it was because he knocked her up," Gene interjected.

Melba wagged her fork at her husband. "They were in love," she insisted.

"And five months after they got married, they had a baby," Gene told him.

His wife sniffed—likely as much in disapproval of the fact as her husband's recitation of gossip. "What matters is that they're together now and a family with their little girl."

"Speaking of little girls," Trey said, looking at his cousin's daughter seated across from him in her high chair. "I can't get over how much this one has grown in the past few months."

"Like a weed," Levi confirmed, ruffling the soft hair on the top of his daughter's head.

Bekka looked up at him, her big blue eyes wide and adoring.

"No doubt that one's a daddy's girl," Claire noted.

Her husband just grinned.

"Speaking of Kayla Dalton," his grandmother said.

"Who was speaking of Kayla Dalton?" Gene asked.

"Trey was," Melba said.

"We were talking about Bekka."

"Earlier," Melba clarified. "When I mentioned the Dalton girl got engaged, he asked if it was Kayla."

"Hers was just the first name that came to mind," Trey hastened to explain.

"And I wonder why that was," his grandmother mused.

"Probably because he was up close and personal with her at Braden and Jennifer's wedding," Claire teased.

"Anyway," Melba interjected. "I was wondering if you were going to see Kayla while you're in town."

"I already did," he admitted. "She walked by the community center when we were unloading the truck."

His grandmother shook her head as she began to stack the empty plates. "I meant, are you going to go out with her?"

"Melba," her husband said warningly.

"What? Is there something wrong with wanting my grandson to spend time with a nice girl?"

Claire pushed away from the table to help clear it.

"Kayla is a nice girl," Trey confirmed. "But if you've got matchmaking on your mind, you're going to be disappointed—I'm not looking to settle down yet, not with anybody."

"And even if he was, Kayla is hardly his type," Claire noted.

Levi's brows lifted. "Trey has a type?"

"Well, if he did, it wouldn't be the shy wallflower type," his wife said.

"Still waters run deep," their grandmother noted.

"What's that supposed to mean?" Trey asked warily.

"It means that there's a lot more to that girl than most people realize," Melba said, setting an enormous apple pie on the table.

Claire brought in the dessert plates and forks.

"And ice cream," her grandmother said. "Bekka's going to want some ice cream."

"I think Bekka wants her bath and bed more than she wants ice cream," Claire said, noting her daughter's drooping eyelids.

"Goodness, she's falling asleep in her chair."

"My fault," Levi said, pushing his chair away from the table and lifting his daughter from hers. "She missed her nap today when I took her to story time at the library."

"Didn't I tell you to put her down as soon as you got back?" Claire asked.

"You did," he confirmed. "But every time I put her in her crib, she started to fuss."

"Why don't you give in to me whenever I fuss?" his wife wanted to know.

He kissed her softly. "Are you saying I don't?"

"Not *all* the time," she said, a small smile on her lips as they headed out of the dining room.

"I guess they've worked things out," Trey mused, stabbing his fork into the generous slab of pie his grandmother set in front of him.

"I really think they have," Melba confirmed. "There will still be bumps in the road—no relationship is ever without them—but over the past few months, they've proven that they are committed to one another and their family."

"If the kid doesn't want ice cream, no one else gets ice cream?" Gene grumbled, frowning at his naked pie.

"You don't need ice cream," his wife told him.

"You didn't need those new gloves you came home with when you were out Christmas shopping last week, but you bought them anyway."

Trey fought against a smile as he got up to get the ice cream. His grandparents' bickering was as familiar to him as the boarding house. They were both strong-willed and stubborn but, even after almost sixty years of marriage, there was an obvious affection between them that warmed his heart.

After they'd finished dessert, his grandmother asked, "So what are your plans for the evening?"

"Do they still show movies at the high school on Fridays?" Trey had spent more than a few evenings in the gymnasium, hanging with his friends or snuggling up to a pretty girl beneath banners that declared, "Go Grizzlies!" and had some fond memories of movie nights at the high school.

"Friday *and* Saturday nights now," she told him.

"Two movie nights a week?" he teased. "And people say there's nothing to do in Rust Creek Falls."

His grandmother narrowed her gaze. "We might not have all the fancy shops and services like Thunder Canyon, but we've got everything we need."

"You're right," he said. "I shouldn't have implied that this town was lacking in any way—especially when two of my favorite people in the world live here."

She swatted him away with her tea towel. "Go on with you now. Take a shower, put on a nice shirt and get out of here."

Trey did as he was told, not only to please his grand-mother but because it occurred to him that the high school was likely where Kayla and Natalie were headed.

Chapter Three

Kayla gazed critically at her reflection in the mirror and sighed as she tugged her favorite Henley-style shirt over her head again and relegated it to the too-tight pile. The nine pounds she'd gained were wreaking havoc with her wardrobe.

Of course, it didn't help that most of the styles were slim-fitting and she was no longer slim. Not that she was fat or even visibly pregnant, but it was apparent that she'd put on some weight, and covering her body in oversize garments at least let her disguise the fact that the weight was all in her belly.

She picked up the Henley again, pulled it on, then put on a burgundy-and-navy plaid shirt over the top. Deciding that would work, she fixed her ponytail, dabbed on some lip gloss and grabbed her keys.

"Where are you going tonight?" her mother asked when Kayla came down the stairs.

She'd mentioned her plans at dinner—when she'd asked her dad if she could take his truck into town—but her mother obviously hadn't been paying attention. Ever since Ryan put a ring on Kristen's finger, her mother had been daydreaming about the wedding.

"I'm meeting Natalie at the high school," she said again. "We're going to see *A Christmas Story* tonight."

"Is it just the two of you going?" her mother pressed.

"No, I'm sure there will be lots of other people there."

"Really, Kayla, I don't know why you can't just give a simple answer to a simple question," Rita chided.

"Sorry," she said automatically. "And yes—it's just me and Natalie tonight. We're not sneaking out to meet boys behind the school."

"Your turn will come."

"My turn for what?" She was baffled by the uncharacteristically gentle tone as much as the words.

"To meet somebody."

"I'm not worried about meeting somebody or not meeting somebody," she assured her mother.

"I had sisters, too," Rita said. "I know it's hard when exciting things are happening in their lives and not your own."

"I'm happy for Kristen, Mom. Genuinely and sincerely."

"Well, of course you are," she agreed. "But that doesn't mean you can't be a little envious, too." A career wife and mother, Rita couldn't imagine her daughters wanting anything else.

She'd been appalled by Kristen's desire to study theater—worried about her daughter associating with unsavory movie people. She'd been so relieved when her youngest child graduated and moved back home to teach drama. Unfortunately, Kristen had faced numerous roadblocks in her efforts to get a high school production off the ground, causing her to turn her attention to the community theater in Kalispell.

Kayla was actually surprised their mother had approved of Kristen's engagement to a Hollywood lawyer. But Ryan had fallen in love with Montana as well as Kristen and was planning to give up his LA practice—as his sister, Maggie, had done just last year when she moved to Rust Creek Falls to marry Jesse Crawford.

But, of course, now that Kristen and Ryan were engaged, it was only natural—to Rita's way of thinking—that Kayla would want the same thing. Her mother would be shocked to learn that her other daughter's life was already winding down a very different path.

"Getting out tonight will be good for you," Rita said to Kayla now. "Who knows? You might even meet someone at the movies."

Meet someone? Ha! She already knew everyone in Rust Creek Falls, and even if she did meet someone new and interesting who actually asked her to go out on a date with him, there was no way she could say yes. Because there was no way she could start a romance with another man while she was carrying Trey's baby.

And no way could she be interested in anyone else when she was still hopelessly infatuated with the father of her child.

"I'm meeting Natalie," she said again. Then, before her mother could say anything else to continue the excruciating conversation, Kayla kissed her cheek. "Don't wait up."

When Kayla arrived, Natalie was standing outside the main doors, her hands stuffed into the pockets of her coat, her feet—tucked into a sleek pair of high-heeled boots that looked more fashionable than warm—kicking the soft snow.

"Am I late?" Kayla asked.

"No, I was probably early," Natalie admitted. "I needed to get out of the house and away from all the talk about weddings."

She nodded her understanding as she reached for the door handle. Natalie's brother had also recently gotten engaged. "When are Brad and Margot getting married?"

"That was one of the topics of discussion. Of course, Brad was married before, so he just wants whatever Margot wants. But Margot lost her mother almost three years ago, and her father's been AWOL since the infamous poker game, so as much as she's excited about starting a life with my brother, I think it's hard for her to be excited about the wedding, and I don't think my mother's being very sensitive about that."

"Believe me, I understand about insensitive mothers," Kayla told her friend.

They paid their admission at the table set up in the foyer for that purpose then made their way toward the gymnasium.

"I always get such a creepy feeling of déjà vu when I'm in here," her friend admitted.

"I know what you mean," Kayla agreed. "It doesn't help that Mrs. Newman—" their freshman physical education teacher "—works at the concession stand."

Natalie nodded her agreement. "Even when I count out the exact change for her, she gives me that perpetual look of disapproval, like I've just told her I forgot my gym clothes."

Kayla laughed. She was glad she'd let her friend drag her out tonight. Not that much dragging was required. Kayla had been feeling in a bit of a funk and had happily accepted Natalie's invitation. Of course, it didn't hurt that

A Christmas Story was one of her all-time favorite holiday movies.

"Oh, look," she said, pointing to the poster advertising a different feature for Saturday night. "We could come back tomorrow for *The Santa Clause*."

"Well, I'm free," Natalie admitted. "Which tells a pretty sad tale about my life."

"Actually, I'm not," Kayla realized.

"Hot date?"

"Ha. I'm helping out at the theater in Kalispell tomorrow night."

"Well, even working in the city has to be more exciting than a night off in this town," Natalie said. Then she stopped dead in her tracks. "Oh. My. God."

"What?" Kayla demanded, as alarmed by her friend's whispered exclamation as the way Natalie's fingers dug into her arm.

"Trey Strickland is here."

Her heart leaped and crashed against her ribs as she turned in the direction her friend was looking.

Yep, it was him.

Not that she really believed Natalie might have been mistaken, but she'd hoped. After a four-month absence, she'd now run into him twice within hours of his return to town. Whether his appearance here was a coincidence or bad luck, it was an obvious sign to Kayla that she wouldn't be able to avoid him while he was in Rust Creek Falls.

Natalie waved a hand in front of her face, fanning herself as she kept her attention fixed on the ginger-haired, broad-shouldered cowboy. "That man is *so* incredibly yummy."

Kayla had always thought so, too—even before she'd experienced the joy of being held in his arms, kissed by his lips, pleasured by his body. But she had no intention of sharing any of that with her friend, who she hadn't realized harbored her own crush on the same man. "Should we get popcorn?" she asked instead.

"I'd rather have man candy," Natalie said dreamily.

Kayla pulled a ten-dollar bill out of the pocket of her too-tight jeans and tried to ignore the reason her favorite denim—and all of her other clothes—were fitting so snugly in recent days. "I'm going for popcorn."

"Can you grab me a soda, too?" Natalie asked, her gaze still riveted on the sexy cowboy as he made his way toward the gym doors.

"Sure."

"I'll go find seats," her friend said, following Trey.

Kayla just sighed and joined the line for concessions. She couldn't blame her friend for being interested, especially when she'd never told Natalie what had happened with Trey on the Fourth of July, but that didn't mean she wanted to be around while the other woman made a play for him.

When she entered the gymnasium with the drinks and popcorn, she found Natalie in conversation with Trey. Though her instinct was to turn in the opposite direction, she forced her feet to move toward them.

Trey's gaze shifted to her and his lips curved. "Hi, again."

"Hi," she echoed his greeting, glancing around. "Are you here with someone?"

Please, let him be here with someone.

But the universe ignored her plea, and Trey shook his head.

"Why don't you join us?" Natalie invited, patting the empty chair on her left.

"I think I will," he said, just as an elderly couple moved toward the two vacant seats beside Natalie.

Trey stepped back, relinquishing the spot she had offered to him. Kayla didn't even have time to exhale a sigh of relief before he moved to the empty seat on the other side of *her*.

She was secretly relieved that her friend's obvious maneuverings had been thwarted, but she didn't know how she would manage to focus on the screen and forget that he was sitting right beside her for the next ninety-four minutes.

In fact, she didn't even make it through four minutes, because she couldn't take a breath without inhaling his clean, masculine scent. She couldn't shift in her seat without brushing against him. And she couldn't stop thinking about the fact that her naked body had been entwined with his.

She forced her attention back to the screen, to the crowd gathered around the window of Higbee's Department Store to marvel at the display of mechanized electronic joy and, of course, Ralphie, wide-eyed and slack-jawed as he fixated on "the holy grail of Christmas gifts—the Red Ryder two hundred shot range model air rifle."

"Are you going to share that popcorn?" Trey whispered close to her ear.

"I am sharing it," she said. "With Natalie."

But deeply ingrained good manners had her shifting the bag to offer it to him.

"Thanks." He dipped his hand inside.

She tried to keep her attention on the movie, but it was no use. Even Ralphie's entertaining antics weren't capable of distracting her from Trey's presence. It was as if every nerve ending in her body was attuned to his nearness.

It probably didn't help that they were in the high school—the setting of so many of her youthful fantasies. So many times she'd stood at her locker and watched him walk past with a group of friends, her heart racing as she waited for him to turn and look at her. So many times she'd witnessed him snuggled up to a cheerleader on the bleachers, and she'd imagined that she was that cheerleader.

Back then, she would have given almost anything to be in the circle of his arms. She would have given almost anything to have him just smile at her. She'd been so seriously and pathetically infatuated that just an acknowledgment of her presence would have fueled her fantasies for days, weeks, months.

When his family had moved away from Rust Creek Falls, she'd cried her heart out. But even then, she'd continued to daydream, imagining that he would come back one day, unable to live without her. She might have been shy and quiet, but deep inside, she was capable of all the usual teenage melodrama—and more.

Sitting beside him now, in the darkened gym, was a schoolgirl fantasy come to life. But he wasn't just sitting in the chair beside her, he was so close that his thigh was pressed against hers. And when he reached into the bag of popcorn she was holding, his fingertips trailed deliberately over the back of her hand.

At least she assumed it was deliberate, because he didn't pull his hand away, even when her breath made an audible catch in her throat.

Natalie glanced at her questioningly.

She cleared her throat, as if there was something stuck in it, and picked up her soda.

She felt a flutter in her tummy that she dismissed as butterflies—a far too usual occurrence when she was around Trey. Then she realized it was their baby—the baby he didn't know about—and her eyes inexplicably filled with tears.

You have to tell him.

The words echoed in the back of her mind, an unending reel of admonishment, the voice of her own conscience in tandem with her sister's.

He has a right to know.

You-have-to-tell-him-he-has-a-right-to-know-you-have-to-tell-him-he-has-a-right-to-know-you-have-to—

"Excuse me," she whispered, thrusting the bag of popcorn at Trey and slipping out of her seat to escape from the gymnasium.

The bright lights of the hallway blinded her for a moment, so that she didn't know which way to turn. She'd spent four years in these halls, but suddenly she couldn't remember the way to the girls' bathroom.

She leaned back against the wall for a minute to get her bearings, then made her way across the hall. Thankfully, the facility was empty, and she slipped into the nearest stall, locked the door, sat down on the closed toilet seat and let the tears fall.

In recent weeks, her emotions had been out of control. She'd been tearing up over the silliest things—a quick glimpse of an elderly couple holding hands, the sight of a mother pushing her child in a stroller, even coffee commercials on TV could start the waterworks. Crying in public bathrooms hadn't exactly become a habit, but this wasn't the first time for her, either.

No, the first time had been three months earlier. After purchasing a pregnancy test from an out-of-the-way pharmacy in Kalispell, she'd driven to the shopping center and taken her package into the bathroom. Because no way could she risk taking the test home, into her parents' house, and then disposing of it—regardless of the result—with the rest of the family's trash.

She remembered every minute of that day clearly. The way her fingers had trembled as she tore open the box, how the words had blurred in front of her eyes as she read and re-read the instructions to make sure she did everything correctly.

After she'd managed to perform the test as indicated, she'd put the stick aside—on the back of the toilet—and counted down the seconds on her watch. When the time was up, she picked up the stick again and looked in the little window, the tears no longer blurring her eyes but sliding freely down her cheeks.

She hadn't bothered to brush them away. She couldn't have stopped them if she'd tried. Never, in all of her twenty-five years, had she imagined being in this situation. Pregnant. Unmarried.

Alone.

She was stunned and scared and completely overwhelmed.

And she was angry. At both herself and Trey for being careless. She didn't know what he'd been thinking, but she'd been so caught up in the moment that she'd forgotten all about protection until he was inside of her. Realization seemed to have dawned on him at the same time, because he'd immediately pulled out of her, apologizing to her, promising that he didn't have unprotected sex—ever.

Then he'd found a condom and covered himself with it before he joined their bodies together again. She didn't know if it was that brief moment of unprotected penetration that had resulted in her pregnancy, or if it was just a statistical reality—if she was one of the two percent of women who was going to be a mommy because condoms were only ninety-eight percent effective in preventing pregnancy.

Of course, the reason didn't matter as much as the reality: she was pregnant. She didn't tell anyone because she didn't know what to say. She didn't know how she felt about the situation—because it was easier to think about her pregnancy as a situation than a baby.

She found an obstetrician in Kalispell—because there was no way she could risk seeing a local doctor—and then, eighteen weeks into her pregnancy, she had an ultrasound.

Everything changed for her then. Looking at the monitor, seeing the image of her unborn child inside of her, made the existence of that child suddenly and undeniably real. That was when she finally accepted that she wasn't just pregnant—the unexpected consequence of an impulsive night in Trey's bed—she was going to have a baby.

Trey's baby.

And in that moment, when she first saw the tiny heart beating, she fell in love with their child.

But he still didn't have a clue about the consequences of the night they'd spent together—or possibly even that they had spent the night together— and she'd resolved to tell him as soon as possible. He had a right to know about their baby. She didn't know how he would respond to the news, but she knew that he needed to hear it.

Of course, at the time of her ultrasound, he'd been in Thunder Canyon, three hundred miles away. So she'd decided to wait until he came back to Rust Creek Falls. And another three-and-a-half weeks had passed. Now he was here—not just in town but in the same building. And she had no more excuses.

She had to tell him about their baby.

She pulled a handful of toilet paper from the roll and wiped at the wet streaks on her cheeks. The tiny life inside her stirred again. She laid a hand on the slight curve of her tummy.

I've always tried to do what I think is best for you, even when I don't know what that is. And I'm scared, because I don't know how your daddy's going to react to the news that he's going to be a daddy. I will tell him. I promise, I will. But I'm not going to walk into the high school gym in the middle of movie night and make a public announcement, so you're going to have to be patient a little longer.

Of course, there was no way the baby could hear the words of reassurance that were audible only inside of her head, but the flutters inside her belly settled.

"Everything okay?" Natalie whispered, when Kayla had returned to her seat inside the darkened gym.

She nodded. "My phone was vibrating, so I went outside to take the call."

Lying didn't come easily to her, but it was easier with her gaze riveted on the movie screen. Thankfully, Natalie accepted her explanation without any further questions.

When the credits finally rolled, people began to stand up and stack their chairs. Trey solicitously took both Kayla's and Natalie's along with his own.

"I'm sorry," Kayla said to her friend, taking advantage of his absence to apologize—although she wasn't really sorry.

"For what?"

"Because I know you wanted to sit next to him."

Natalie waved away the apology. "*I* should be sorry," she said. "When I invited him to join us, I completely forgot that you two were together at the wedding—"

"We weren't together," Kayla was quick to interject.

"Even the Rust Creek Rambler saw the two of you on the dance floor."

"One dance doesn't equal together."

"Well, even if that's true—" and her friend's tone warned Kayla that she wasn't convinced it was "—I'm getting the impression that Trey is hoping for something more."

She shook her head. "You're imagining things."

"I am *not* imagining the way he's looking at you," Natalie said, her gaze shifting beyond her friend.

Kayla didn't know what to say to that. She didn't know how—or even if—Trey was looking at her because she was deliberately avoiding looking at him, afraid that any kind of eye contact would somehow give away all of her secrets to him.

"Which means I have to find myself a different cowboy," Natalie decided.

"Do you have anyone specific in mind?" Kayla asked, happy to shift the conversation away from Trey—and especially talk of the two of them being together at the wedding.

"I'm willing to consider all possibilities," Natalie said. "And since it's still pretty early, why don't we go to the Ace in the Hole to grab a drink?"

She shuddered at the thought. "Because that place on a Friday night is a bad idea."

The local bar and grill was more than a little rough around the edges at the best of times—and a Friday night was never the best of times as the cowboys who worked so hard during the week on the local ranches believed in partying just as hard on the weekends. As a result, it wasn't unusual for tempers to flare and fists to fly, and Kayla had no interest in that kind of drama tonight.

Natalie sighed. "You're right—how about a hot chocolate instead?"

That offer was definitely more tempting. Though Kayla hadn't experienced many cravings, and thankfully nothing too unusual, the baby had definitely shown signs in recent weeks of having a sweet tooth, and she knew that hot chocolate would satisfy that craving. But, "I thought you had to open up the store in the morning."

Natalie waved a hand dismissively. "Morning is a long time away."

"Hot chocolate sounds good," she admitted.

"It tastes even better," Trey said from behind her.

Kayla thought he'd left the gym after helping to stack the chairs, but apparently that had been wishful thinking on her part.

"But where can you get hot chocolate in town at this time of night?" he asked.

"Daisy's," Natalie told him. "It's open late now, with an expanded beverage menu and pastries to encourage people to stay in town rather than heading to the city."

"I always did like their hot chocolate," Trey said. "Do you mind if I join you?"

"Of course not," Natalie said, buttoning up her coat as they exited the gym.

They said "hello" to various townspeople as they passed them in the halls, stopping on the way to chat with some other friends from high school. A few guys invited Trey to go for a beer at the Ace in the Hole, but he told them that he already had plans. When they finally made their escape, Natalie pulled her phone out of her pocket and frowned at the time displayed on the screen. "I didn't realize it was getting to be so late."

Kayla narrowed her gaze on her friend, wondering how it had gone from "still pretty early" to "so late" in the space of ten minutes.

"I think I should skip the hot chocolate tonight," Natalie decided. "I have to be up early to open the store in the morning."

"You were the one who suggested it," Kayla pointed out.

"I know," her friend agreed. "And I hate to bail, but there's no reason that you and Trey can't go without me."

Kayla glanced at Trey. "Wouldn't you rather go to the Ace in the Hole with your friends than to Daisy's with me?"

"Let me see—reminiscing about high school football with a bunch of washed-up jocks or making conversation with a pretty girl?" He winked at her. "It seems like a no-brainer to me."

"Great," Natalie said, a little too enthusiastically.

Then she leaned in to give Kayla a quick hug and whisper in her ear. "I'll call you tomorrow to hear all of the juicy details, so make sure there *are* some juicy details."

Chapter Four

"She's not very subtle, is she?" Trey asked Kayla, after her friend had gone.

"Not at all," she agreed. "And if you want to skip the hot chocolate—"

"I don't want to skip the hot chocolate," he told her.

"Okay."

It was one little word—barely two syllables—which made it hard for him to read her tone to know what she was thinking. But her spine was stiff and her hands stuffed deep in the pockets of her jacket, clear indications that she was neither behind her friend's machinations nor pleased by them.

"Do *you* want to skip the hot chocolate?" he asked her.

Her hesitation was so brief it was barely noticeable before she replied, "I never say no to hot chocolate."

Despite her words, he suspected that she wanted to but couldn't think of a way to graciously extricate herself from the situation that had been set up by her friend.

Was she avoiding him? Was she uneasy because of what had happened between them in the summer? He couldn't blame her if she was, especially since they hadn't ever talked about that night. Not since that first day, anyway, before he'd had a chance to really remember what happened.

He didn't want her to feel uncomfortable around him. Aside from the fact that her brother was one of his best friends, Rust Creek Falls was a small town, and it was inevitable that they would bump into one another. For that reason alone, they needed to clear the air between them.

"I'd offer to drive, but I walked over," he told her.

His grandparents' boarding house being centrally located, there wasn't anything in the town that wasn't within walking distance. Which included Daisy's Donuts, only a block over from the high school.

"We'll go in my truck," she said, because driving was preferable to walking even that short distance in the frigid temperatures that prevailed in Montana in December.

She unlocked the doors with the electronic key fob, and he followed her to the driver's side and opened the door to help her in. It was a big truck, and she had to step up onto the running board first. He cupped her elbow, to ensure she didn't lose her balance, and she murmured a quiet "Thanks."

By the time he'd buckled himself into the passenger side, she had the truck in gear. Either she was really craving hot chocolate or she didn't want to be alone with him for a minute longer than necessary. He suspected it was the latter.

He wasn't sure if she was sending mixed signals or if he was just having trouble deciphering them. When he'd stepped out of the community center earlier that afternoon and saw her walking past, he'd been sincerely pleased to see her. His blood had immediately heated and his heart had pounded hard and fast inside his chest. And he'd thought that she was happy to see him, too.

In that first moment, when their eyes had met, he was sure there had been a spark in her blue gaze and a smile on her lips. Then her smile had faltered, as if she wasn't sure that she should be happy to see him. Which confirmed to him that they needed to talk about the Fourth of July.

As she parked in front of Daisy's Donuts, he realized this probably wasn't the place to do so. Not unless they wanted to announce their secret to all of Rust Creek Falls, which he was fairly certain neither of them did.

"Why don't you grab a table while I get our drinks?" he suggested.

"Okay," she agreed.

"Any special requests?" He glanced at the board. "Dark chocolate? White chocolate? Peppermint? Caramel?"

"Regular," she said. "With extra whipped cream."

"You got it."

He decided to have the same and added a couple of gingerbread cookies to the order, too.

"I thought you might be hungry," he told her, setting the plate of cookies between them. "Considering that I ate all of your popcorn."

"I'm not hungry," she said, accepting the mug he slid across the table to her. "But I love gingerbread cookies. My mother used to make a ton of them at Christmastime, but there were never any left when company came over because Kristen and I used to sneak down to the kitchen and eat all of them."

"You said she used to make them," he noted. "She doesn't anymore?"

"She makes us do it now. She decided that since we eat most of them anyway, we should know how to make them."

He nudged the plate toward her, silently urging her to take a cookie. She broke the leg off one, popped it into her mouth.

"Good?"

She nodded.

"My grandmother used to make gingerbread houses—one for each of the grandkids to decorate. When I think back, she must have spent a fortune on candy, and we ate more than we put on the buildings." He broke a piece off the other cookie, sampled it. "I wonder if she'd make one for me this year, if I asked."

"I'm sure she'd make anything you wanted," Kayla said.

"What makes you say that?" he asked curiously.

"Three words." She broke off the gingerbread boy's other leg. "Vanilla almond fudge."

He smiled, thinking of the plate he'd found on his bedside table—neatly wrapped in plastic and tied with a bow. "She does spoil me," he admitted.

Kayla smiled back, and their eyes held for a brief second before she quickly dropped her gaze away.

The group of teenagers who had been sitting nearby got up from their table, put on their coats, hats and gloves and headed out the door. There were still other customers around, but no one close enough that he needed to worry about their conversation being overheard.

"Did I do something wrong?"

She looked up again. "What are you talking about?"

"I'm not sure," he admitted. "But I get the feeling that you're not very happy to see me back in town."

She sipped her cocoa and shrugged. "Your coming back doesn't have anything to do with me."

"Maybe it does," he said. "Because I haven't stopped thinking about you since I left Rust Creek Falls in the summer."

She blinked. "You haven't?"

"I haven't," he confirmed, holding her gaze.

"Oh."

He waited a beat, but she didn't say anything more. "It would be nice to hear that you've thought about me, too…if you have."

She glanced away, color filling her cheeks. "I have."

"And the night of the wedding?" he prompted.

He watched, intrigued, as the pink in her cheeks deepened.

"You mean the night we were both drinking the spiked punch?" she asked.

"Is that the only reason you started talking to me that night?"

"Probably," she admitted. "I mean—I would have wanted to talk to you, but I wouldn't have had the nerve to start a conversation."

"And the kiss? Was that because of the punch, too?"

"*You* kissed *me*," she said indignantly.

"You kissed back pretty good," he told her.

She remained silent, probably because she couldn't deny it.

"And then you went back to my room with me," he prompted further.

She nodded slowly, almost reluctantly.

"Are you sorry that you did?"

She kept her gaze averted from his, but she shook her head.

"I'm not sorry, either," he told her. "The only thing I regret is that it took me so long to remember what happened."

"Lots of people had memory lapses after that night— because of the punch," she said.

"Do you really think that what happened between us only happened because of the punch?"

"Don't you?"

He frowned at her question. "I don't know how drunk *you* were, but I can assure you, there isn't enough alcohol in the world to make me get naked with a woman I'm not attracted to."

Her perfectly arched brows drew together. "You were attracted…to me?"

"Why do you find that so hard to believe?"

"I'm the quiet one. Kristen's the pretty one."

"You're identical twins."

She lifted a shoulder. "You seem to be able to tell us apart."

"There are some subtle differences," he acknowledged. "Your eyes are a little bit darker, your bottom lip is just a little bit fuller and you have a mole on the top of your left earlobe."

"I never would have guessed you were so observant," she said, blushing a little.

"I didn't realize how much I observed you," he admitted. "Are you worried now that I'm a stalker?"

She shook her head. "No, I'm not worried you're a stalker."

"Then you should trust me when I say that you're a beautiful woman, Kayla. Beautiful, sweet, smart and sexy."

"Sexy?"

"*Incredibly* sexy," he assured her.

She folded her arms over her chest. "Is *that* what this is about?"

"What?" he asked warily.

"You figure that since I fell into your bed so easily that

night, I'd be eager to do so again. Is that the real reason you wanted to see me?"

He held up his hands as his head spun with the effort of following her convoluted logic. "Whoa! Wait a minute."

"*You* wait a minute," she said. "I'm not so pathetic that I'm willing to go home with any guy who says a few kind words to me."

His jaw dropped. "*What* are you talking about?"

"I'm talking about your apparent effort to lure me back into your bed."

"*I* didn't lure you the first time," he reminded her. "*You* were the one who approached me at the wedding. *You* were the one who rubbed your body against mine on the dance floor. And *you* were the one who said you'd go back to my room with me."

She dropped her face into her hands. "Ohmygod—I did do all of that, didn't I? It was all my fault."

Her reaction seemed a little extreme to him, but she sounded so distraught, he couldn't help wanting to console her. "I'm not sure there's any need to assign blame," he said. "Especially considering that I didn't object to any of it."

"I really am pathetic."

He reached across the table and pulled her hands away from her face. "No, you're not."

"I am," she insisted. "I had such a crush on you in high school."

"You did?"

"And you didn't even know I existed."

"I knew you existed," he said. "But you were Derek's little sister."

She nodded. "And I guess…when you asked me to dance… I got caught up in the high school fantasy again."

"You had fantasies about me?" He was intrigued by the possibility.

"You played the starring role in all of my romantic dreams."

"I'm flattered," he told her sincerely. "But why are you telling me this now?"

Why was *she telling him this*? Kayla asked herself the same question.

Because she was nervous, and she always babbled when she was nervous. Of course, now that she'd confided in him about her schoolgirl crush, she could add *mortified* to the list of emotions that were clouding her brain.

"I'm trying to explain…and apologize."

"I don't want an apology."

"But I threw myself at you," she said miserably.

And, as a result of her actions, she was now pregnant with his baby. Which was what she was trying to work up to telling him, but she was sure that when she did, he would hate her—and she really didn't want him to hate her.

"It wasn't like that at all," he assured her. "And even if it was, I was happy to catch you."

"I don't usually…do what I did that night."

Trey was quiet for a minute before he finally said, "It seems obvious that you think that night was a mistake, and your brother would undoubtedly agree—after he pounded on me for taking advantage of you. And while I'm sorry you feel that way, I have no intention of telling anyone about what happened between us, if that's what you're worried about. As far as I'm concerned, it will be our little secret, okay?"

His speech left her speechless. The words that Kayla had been struggling to put together into a coherent sentence faded from her mind. Tears clogged her throat, burned her eyes, as she shook her head.

"I'm not sure that's possible," she admitted.

"You told somebody about that night?" he guessed.

She nodded. "My sister."

"Oh." He considered for a minute, then let out a weary sigh. "Well, I'm sure you can trust your sister to keep your secrets. Unless…"

"Unless what?"

"I've heard some speculation that she's the Rust Creek Rambler," he admitted.

"She's not."

"You're sure?"

"I'm sure," she confirmed. "If she was the Rambler, I would know."

"Then our secret is safe," he said again.

She thought about the baby she carried, the tiny life that was even now fluttering in her belly. She'd managed to keep her pregnancy a secret from everyone—even her own family—for months. But she'd put on nine pounds already, and the bulky sweaters she'd been wearing wouldn't hide the baby bump for much longer.

You have to tell Trey.

She opened her mouth to do so when her cousin, Caleb, came in with his wife, Mallory. They waved a greeting across the room before stepping up to the counter to order their drinks.

When they took their beverages to the table behind Kayla and Trey, she knew that the opportunity to tell him about her pregnancy had slipped away.

RUST CREEK RAMBLINGS: LIGHTS! CAMERAS! ACTIVIST!

Lily Dalton, the town's littlest matchmaker (though

certainly not the only one!) has turned her talents toward a new vocation: acting. But when the sign-up sheet was posted for auditions for the elementary school's production of *The Nutcracker*, the precocious third-grader refused to succumb to gender stereotypes. Uninterested in the traditional female parts, she insisted on auditioning for the title role—and won! The revised tale will undoubtedly be the highlight of this year's holiday pageant...

"I can't believe I had to hear about your date with Trey Strickland from Natalie Crawford," Kristen grumbled. "Why didn't you tell me?"

"It wasn't a date," Kayla pointed out. "And I didn't have a chance to tell you, because this is the first time you've been home since Friday night."

"You could have called or texted."

She could have, of course, but she hadn't been ready to talk to her sister about it. The shock of seeing Trey so unexpectedly had churned up all kinds of emotions, and she needed some time to sift through them before she could talk about them. Unfortunately, the thirty-six hours that had passed since then still hadn't been nearly enough.

"It wasn't that big a deal," she hedged.

Kristen's brows lifted. "The father of your baby is back in town—I think that's a pretty big deal."

Kayla pushed her bedroom door closed. "Can you please keep your voice down?"

"Everyone is downstairs having breakfast."

"Which is where we should be, too," Kayla said. "And if we don't go down, Mom's going to come up here looking for us."

"We'll go down in a minute," Kristen said. "I want

to know how many times you've seen Trey since he got back."

"Once."

Her sister's gaze narrowed.

"Okay, twice," she acknowledged. "But they were both the same day."

"Did you tell him?"

"No."

"Why not?"

"Because I didn't know how."

"It's only two words—I'm pregnant."

Kristen made it sound so easy, as if Kayla was making it harder than it needed to be. And maybe she was. But she was the one who had to find the right time and place to say those two words, and she didn't appreciate being bullied by her sister.

She blinked back the tears that threatened. "And on that note, I'm going down for breakfast."

Kristen reached out and touched her arm, halting her departure.

"I'm sorry," she said softly, sincerely. "It's just that I can see how this is tearing you up inside, and it's going to continue tearing you up until you find a way to tell Trey— and that's not good for you or the baby."

"I know," she admitted.

"Besides, I saw an adorable little bib the other day that read, 'If you think I'm cute, you should see my aunt,' and I want to be able to buy things like that and bring them home for your baby."

Kayla managed a smile. "You're going to spoil this kid rotten before it's even born, aren't you?"

"I'm going to try," Kristen confirmed.

They left the room together, Kayla feeling confident

that whatever happened with Trey, her baby was going to be surrounded by the love and support of her family.

Trey decided that he wanted to see Kayla again more than he wanted to play it cool. Besides, what was the point in waiting a few days to call when it only wasted a few days of the short time that he was in town?

She answered the phone with a tentative hello—obviously not recognizing his number. But even hearing her voice say that one word was enough to make him smile.

"I was hoping to take you out for dinner tonight."

She paused. "Trey?"

"Yeah, it's me," he confirmed. "Are you free?"

"Oh. Um. Actually, I'm not," she said. "I'm on my way to Kalispell with my sister."

"What's in Kalispell?"

"*A Christmas Carol.*"

"Another movie?"

"No, the play. Kristen is Ebenezer Scrooge's fiancée, Belle."

"I didn't know Scrooge was married."

"He wasn't. She ended their relationship when she realized he loved money more than he loved her."

"I don't remember that part of the story," he admitted.

"Maybe you should buy a ticket to see it onstage, to refresh your memory."

"Would you go with me?"

"I've seen it a dozen times already from the wings."

"Is that a yes?"

She laughed softly. "No."

"Okay—what are you doing tomorrow?"

"I don't have any specific plans," she admitted.

"Can I take you out for lunch?"

She hesitated, and he wondered if she was searching for

another excuse to say no. And if she did, then he should finally take the hint and stop asking. He wasn't in the habit of chasing women, and he wasn't going to sacrifice his pride—and his relationship with Derek—to chase after his friend's little sister.

But when she finally responded, it was to say, "That would be nice."

"I'll pick you up at noon."

"I'll meet you," she said quickly.

"You don't want me coming to the ranch?" he guessed.

"I just don't think there's any reason for you to drive all the way out here just to turn around and drive back into town again," she said. "Especially when I have to stop by the newspaper office in the afternoon, anyway."

"Okay," he relented. "Where do you want to meet?"

"How about Daisy's again?"

He made a face that, of course, she couldn't see. But when he mentioned lunch, he was thinking a thick juicy burger or a rack of ribs from the Ace in the Hole. Sure, the donut shop did hot beverages and pastries, but he wanted a real meal. "Do they have much of a lunch menu?"

"I'm sure you'll find something that appeals to you."

He suspected she was right, though he wasn't thinking about the diner's menu.

"Okay, I'll see you at noon tomorrow."

He was smiling when he hung up the phone—then he turned and found his grandmother in his doorway.

"Who are you seeing at noon tomorrow?"

He could hardly take her to task for eavesdropping when he hadn't bothered to close his door. "A friend."

"A female friend, I'd guess, based on the smile on your face."

He focused his attention on the plate in her hands. "Is that sandwich for me?"

"You didn't come down to make anything for yourself, and I didn't want you messing up my kitchen after I'd cleaned it up."

He kissed her cheek. "Thank you."

"Do you have beverages?" Melba asked, glancing toward the mini-fridge in the corner of his room.

"I do," he confirmed. "And chips in the cabinet."

"Don't be getting crumbs all over," she admonished.

"I won't." And he knew where the broom was kept if he did.

She nodded. "Was that the Dalton girl you were talking to?"

"You don't give up, do you?"

"I should give up hoping that my grandson finds a nice girl to spend his life with?"

He held up his hands. "You're getting way ahead of me here," he told her. "I'm talking about lunch, not a lifetime commitment."

"Every relationship has to start somewhere," she said philosophically.

He knew she was right. He also knew it was far too soon to be thinking about anything long-term with Kayla Dalton. They hadn't even been on a real date, and he wasn't sure that their lunch plans even counted as such.

He really liked Kayla. He wasn't sure what it was about her that set her apart from so many other girls that he'd met and dated in recent years. He only knew that he wanted to spend time with her while he was in town and get to know her better.

And yes, he wanted to make love with her again when his brain wasn't clouded by alcohol. He wanted to know if her lips would taste as delicious as he remembered, if her skin would feel as soft beneath his hands, if her body would respond to his as it did in his dreams.

But he was prepared to take things slow this time, to enjoy every step of the journey without racing to the finish. And he was looking forward to lunch being that first step.

Chapter Five

Kayla was waiting for Trey outside the diner when he arrived. She'd dressed appropriately for the weather and looked cute all bundled up in a navy hip-length ski jacket with a knitted pink scarf wrapped around her throat and a matching hat on her head. Her legs were clad in dark denim, her feet tucked into dark brown cowboy boots.

"Busy place," he noted, opening the door for her so they could join the lineup of customers waiting to order at the counter.

"As I'm sure you're aware, dining options are pretty limited around here."

He was aware—and reassured to see a few local ranchers chowing down on hearty-looking sandwiches.

"It doesn't look as if the newlyweds regret their impulsive ceremony or intoxicated nuptials," Kayla noted, nodding toward a table where Will Clifton was sitting with his wife, Jordyn Leigh.

Trey had heard that the couple married on the Fourth of

July while under the influence of the wedding punch, but something about Kayla's choice of words struck a chord— as if he recognized the phrase *intoxicated nuptials* from somewhere.

"I heard a lot of people did crazy things under the influence of that punch," he said.

An elderly woman in a long, purple coat with an orange cap over her gray hair was standing ahead of them in line, and she turned back to face them now. "For some, the repercussions of that night are yet to be revealed."

Trey didn't know what to make of that cryptic comment, but Kayla's cheeks drained of all color.

"What was that about?" he whispered the question to her.

"I have no idea," she said.

"*Who* was that?"

"Winona Cobbs—a self-proclaimed psychic who moved here from Whitehorn a couple years back. Apparently, she used to run a place called the Stop 'N' Swap, but now she writes a nationally syndicated column, *Wisdom by Winona*."

"She's a little scary," he said. "Not just what she said, but the way she said it, as if she knows something that no one else does."

"Some people think she truly has a gift, others think she's a quack."

"What do you think?" he asked.

Kayla's expression was uneasy as she watched Winona settle at an empty table. "I think we should get our lunch to go."

"To go *where*?"

"We can eat in the park," she suggested.

"You want to eat outside?"

"It's a beautiful day," she pointed out.

"It's sunny," he acknowledged. "But the temperature is hovering just above freezing."

"I have a blanket in my car."

He'd been born and raised in Montana and was accustomed to working outside in various weather conditions, but even when the sun was shining, he didn't consider thirty-four degrees to be a beautiful day. But if Kayla could handle being outside, he wasn't going to wimp out.

He ordered a hot roast-beef sandwich platter with fries and slaw; Kayla opted for grilled turkey on a ciabatta bun with provolone and cranberry mayonnaise.

"To go," she told the server.

Trey glanced around the diner. "There are plenty of tables in here," he noted. "Are you sure you want to go to the park?"

"I'm sure."

He carried the bag of food and tray of hot drinks while she retrieved a thick wool blanket from her truck. It was a short walk to the park, where she spread the blanket over the bench seat for them, folding the end back across her lap when she was seated.

Maybe it wasn't exactly a beautiful day, but she looked beautiful in the sunlight. He didn't think she'd ever worn a lot of makeup, but she didn't need it. Those big blue eyes were mesmerizing even without any artificial enhancement; the soft, full lips naturally pink and tempting. She smelled sweet, like vanilla and brown sugar. The scent triggered a fresh wave of memories of the night they'd spent together and stirred his blood. Thankfully, his sheepskin-lined leather jacket was long enough to hide any evidence of his body's instinctive response.

He opened the bag and took out the food, unwrapping Kayla's sandwich so that she didn't have to take off her mittens before turning his attention to his own.

"Thanks."

"You're welcome."

That was the extent of their conversation for a few minutes while they both concentrated on eating. Trey had to admit, his roast beef was delicious. The meat was thinly sliced and piled high on a Kaiser then topped with gravy so piping hot, there was steam coming off his sandwich.

When the sandwich was gone, he turned his attention to the fries—thick wedges of crispy potato that were equally delicious. "Obviously, Daisy's Donuts has a lot more going for it than just donuts these days."

"I told you you'd find something you liked."

"So you did," he agreed.

A gust of wind blew her hair into her face. Kayla lifted a mittened hand to shove it away.

"Your hair looks different today," he noted.

"It's covered by a hat," she pointed out.

"Aside from that."

She shrugged. "I haven't had it cut in a while. It's probably longer than it was in the summer."

He wrapped a strand around his finger, tugged gently. "You wore it pinned up at the wedding."

She nodded.

He remembered taking the pins out of her hair and combing his fingers through the long, silky tresses. Of course, he didn't mention that part to her, because he knew that she was still a little embarrassed about what had happened that night.

"So you mentioned that your sister plays the part of Scrooge's fiancée in *A Christmas Carol*, but you didn't tell me what your role is."

"I work behind the scenes," she told him. "Helping out with costumes, scenery and props."

"So you don't have to be there for every performance?" he guessed.

"No. I usually work Wednesday and Thursday nights, and the occasional Saturday matinee."

"That's a pretty big commitment."

"Kristen does eight shows a week," she noted. "And Belle isn't a major part, but she's also the understudy for Mrs. Cratchit."

Once again, she'd deflected attention away from herself in favor of her twin. Trey noticed that she did that a lot. What he didn't know was if it was because she was proud of her sister or uncomfortable having any attention focused on herself.

Now that he thought about it, she'd always seemed content to hover in Kristen's shadow, but he didn't remember seeing much of her sister on the Fourth of July. "Was Kristen at the wedding?" he asked her now.

"Of course," Kayla responded. "Although she spent most of her time on the dance floor or with Ryan."

"I'm glad she was preoccupied," he said. "Because I don't think you would have approached me if you'd been hanging out with her."

"Probably not," she acknowledged. "But even without Kristen around, I wouldn't have approached you if I hadn't been drinking the spiked punch."

"Then I guess I should say thank you to whoever spiked the punch."

She narrowed her gaze on him, but the sparkle in her blue eyes assured him that she was only teasing when she said, "Maybe it was you."

"The police still haven't found the culprit?"

She shook her head. "No, and I'm not sure they ever will."

"What makes you say that?"

"It's been five months and there's no new evidence, no more leads to follow, no other witnesses to interview."

"What about Boyd Sullivan?" he asked, referring to the old man who had literally bet his ranch in a high-stakes poker game the night of the wedding.

"I'm sure they'd like to talk to him, if they could find him, but I doubt that he's responsible for spiking the punch when that's believed to be the reason he lost his home."

"Some pretty strange things happened that night," he acknowledged. "But it wasn't all bad, was it?"

Kayla knew he was asking about the time they'd spent together, and seeking reassurance that she had no regrets.

"No," she said in response to Trey's question. "It wasn't all bad."

But he didn't know that there were unexpected repercussions from that night, and she had to tell him. There probably wouldn't be a smoother segue into the topic or a more perfect opportunity. She opened her mouth to speak, but the words—those two simple words—stuck in her throat.

Because those two words would only be the beginning of their conversation. Once she told him about their baby, he'd have questions—*a lot* of questions. How could she explain to him how it had happened when she wasn't entirely sure herself? And how could she possibly justify remaining silent about the fact for so long?

"But you wish you hadn't gone back to my room with me?" he guessed.

"No. I just wish…"

"What do you wish?"

She shook her head. "I just want you to know that I don't usually do things like that. At least, I never have before."

He frowned. "You weren't a virgin."

She flushed. "I didn't mean that. I only meant that I've never had a one-night stand before."

"I didn't invite you back to my room with the plan that we would only spend one night together," he told her. "But the next morning, well, you know that I was a little hazy on the details. And you seemed to want to pretend it had never happened, so I decided to play along."

"I thought *you* didn't remember."

"I wouldn't—couldn't—forget making love with you," he told her.

"But you never even looked at me twice before that night."

"That's not true. The truth is, I was always careful not to get caught looking at you, because of my friendship with your brother." He crumpled up his sandwich wrapper, dropped it into the bag. "The punch didn't make me notice you—it only lessened my inhibitions around you."

"Really?"

"Really." He wiped his fingers on a paper napkin. "But maybe you only noticed me because of the punch."

"You know that's not true."

"That's right—the remnants of your high school crush meant I was irresistible to you," he teased.

"Maybe it was the punch," she teased back.

He grinned. "Well, now that you're not under the influence, what do you say to the two of us spending some time together, getting to know one another better?"

Under other circumstances, she would have said "absolutely." She wanted exactly what he was offering, but she knew any time they might have together was limited—not just because he would be returning to Thunder Canyon in the New Year, but because her baby bump was growing every day.

If you don't tell him, I will.

With Kristen's voice echoing in the back of her mind, Kayla opened her mouth to finally confess her secret. "Before you decide that you want—"

"I'm sorry," Trey said, as his cell phone rang. He pulled it out of his pocket, glanced at the screen. "My cousin, Claire."

He looked at her, as if for permission.

"Go ahead," she said, grateful for the reprieve—and then feeling guilty about being grateful.

He connected the call. "Hey, Claire."

Whatever his cousin said on the other end made him wince. "TMI." He shook his head as he listened some more. "So why are you calling me?" Then he sighed. "Okay, text me the details—but that 'favorite cousin' card is wearing pretty thin."

"Problem?" Kayla asked, when he disconnected.

"She wants me to pick up diapers. Apparently, she bought a supersize package at the box store in Kalispell yesterday, but she left them in the car and Levi has the car at work, Grandma's out getting her hair done, she doesn't trust Grandpa to buy the right size and she needs diapers *now*."

"And you didn't even know diapers came in different sizes?" Kayla guessed.

"I never really thought about it," he admitted. "Except about two minutes ago and more in the context of 'thank God I don't have to think about stuff like that.'"

She frowned as she folded up the blanket. "Stuff like what?"

"Any and all of the paraphernalia associated with babies. I swear, you can hardly see the floor in Claire and Levi's room for all of the toys and crap strewn around."

Toys and crap.

Well, that was an enlightening turn of phrase. If she'd

been under any illusions that Trey might be excited about impending fatherhood, the phone call from his cousin had cleared them away.

Thank God I don't have to think about stuff like that.

His phone chimed and he glanced at the screen again. "She actually texted me a picture of the package, to make sure I get the right ones."

"Then I guess you'd better go get the diapers."

"I'm sorry," he said. "She really did sound desperate, although I'll spare you the details that she didn't spare me."

"I have to head over to the newspaper office, anyway," she reminded him. "Thanks for lunch."

"Wait." He caught her arm as she started to move away. "You were in the middle of saying something when Claire called."

She furrowed her brow, as if trying to remember, then shrugged. "I don't remember now."

Liar, liar.

She ignored the recriminations from her conscience as she headed back to her truck.

When she got to the newspaper office and glanced at her own phone, Kayla saw that she had three missed calls and four text messages—all from her sister.

She sat down behind her desk and finally called her back.

"What did he say?" Kristen demanded without pre-amble.

"Hi, Kristen. It's good to hear from you. I'm doing well, thanks for asking, and how are you?"

Her sister huffed out a breath. "We covered all of that when I talked to you earlier. Now tell me what he said."

"I didn't tell him," she admitted.

"How could you not tell him? Wasn't the whole purpose of your meeting with him today to tell him about your baby—*his* baby?"

"Yes, that was the purpose," she agreed. "And I was trying to come up with the right words to tell him what I needed to tell him."

"That you're pregnant with his child."

She sighed. "I'm aware of that fact."

"If you can't even say the words over the phone to me, there's no way you're going to be able to say them to Trey."

"I know," she admitted. "And those words are going to turn his whole world upside down."

"Probably a lot less than the baby that's going to come along in a few more months," Kristen pointed out reasonably.

"Not just a baby, but all the *toys and crap* that go along with a baby."

"What?"

She sighed. "Claire called and asked Trey to pick up diapers for her, and he went off on a little bit of a rant that made it pretty clear he isn't ready to be a father."

"Ready or not—he is going to be one."

"I know," she said again.

"The longer you wait, the harder it's going to be," her sister warned.

She knew it was true. And she knew that she'd already waited too long, but with Trey's disparaging remark ringing in her ears, the truth had lodged in her throat. So many times, she'd tried to imagine how he'd react to the news, but every time she played the scene out in her mind, the mental reel came to a dead stop after she told him about the baby. She simply could not imagine how he would respond. His comments today gave her a little bit of a hint, and not a good one.

"The baby's moving around a lot now," she admitted.

"The whole time I was with Trey today, I could feel little flutters, as if the baby was responding to the sound of his voice."

"Maybe he was," Kristen said. "Or maybe my nephew was kicking at you, reminding you to tell his father about his existence."

"I don't know if the baby's a boy or a girl," she reminded her sister.

"It's a boy," Kristen said. "And a little boy needs his father."

"What if…"

"What if what?"

But Kayla couldn't finish the thought. A single tear leaked out the corner of her eye—not that her sister could see, of course, but in true Kristen fashion, she didn't need to see her to know.

"Are you crying, sweetie?"

"No."

"Kayla," her sister prompted gently.

"One tear is not crying," she protested.

"It's going to be okay," Kristen said. "But only if you tell him."

"What if he doesn't want our baby?" she asked, her voice barely a whisper. "What if he hates me for getting pregnant?"

"You didn't get pregnant alone," her sister said indignantly. "And if he couldn't be responsible enough to make sure that didn't happen, he has to be responsible for the consequences."

RUST CREEK RAMBLINGS: BITS & BITES
The spectacularly refurbished Maverick Manor has been doing steady business since it opened its doors last December. Rumor has it the exquisite honey-

moon suite is in particular demand and has already been booked for the wedding night of dashing detective Russ Campbell to Rust Creek Falls's sexy spitfire waitress, Lani Dalton.

In other news, a truckload of our neighbors from Thunder Canyon recently rode into town bringing Presents for Patriots. The group included DJ and Allaire Traub with their pint-size son, Alex; Shane and Gianna Roarke, who will obviously be adding to their family very soon; Clayton and Antonia Traub, with children Bennett and Lucy in tow; and Trey Strickland, who is apparently planning to spend the holidays with his grandparents. Take my advice, single ladies, and slip a sprig of mistletoe in your pocket just in case you're lucky enough to cross paths with the handsome bachelor while he's in Rust Creek Falls!

Gene folded his newspaper and set it aside. "Better watch out," he told his grandson. "The Rambler announced your return to all of the eligible women in town."

"As if the news hadn't spread farther and faster through the grapevine already," Trey noted.

"Something wrong?" Melba asked him.

"Why would you think that?"

"You've been pushing those eggs around on your plate for five minutes without taking a bite."

He lifted a forkful to his mouth and tried not to make a face as he swallowed the cold eggs.

"I heard about your lunch with Kayla Dalton on Monday," Melba said.

He didn't bother to ask where she'd heard. In a town the size of Rust Creek Falls, everyone knew everyone else's business.

"In the park," she continued, shaking her head. "Why on earth would you take the girl to the park in December?"

"The park was Kayla's idea," he told her.

Melba frowned at that. "Really?"

"And it was a nice day."

"Nice enough, for this time of year," his grandmother agreed. "But hardly nice enough for a picnic."

"You should take her to Kalispell," Gene said.

"Why would I take her to Kalispell?" he asked warily.

"For a proper date."

He looked across the table at his grandfather. "*You're* giving *me* dating advice?"

"Somebody apparently has to," Melba pointed out. "Because lunch in the park in December is *not* a date."

He didn't bother reminding her again that it had been Kayla's idea—clearly nothing he said was going to change her opinion.

"You should take her somewhere nice," his grandmother continued.

"Speaking of going places," he said. "I'm heading to Kalispell this afternoon to do some Christmas shopping. Do you need me to pick up anything for you?"

"I was there to get my groceries yesterday," Melba said. "You should ask Kayla to go with you."

"Grandma," he said, with more than a hint of exasperation in his tone.

She held her hands up in mock surrender. "It was just a suggestion."

And because it was one he was tempted to follow, he instead got up and cleared his plate from the table, then headed out the door.

Chapter Six

The following night Kayla had volunteered to help with the wrapping of Presents for Patriots at the community center. She wasn't surprised to see Trey was also in attendance, but she deliberately took an empty seat at the table closest to the doors—far away from where he was seated.

She wasn't exactly avoiding him, but after the way they'd parted at the conclusion of their lunch date, she wasn't sure of the status between them. She knew that nothing he'd said or done absolved her of the responsibility of telling him about their baby, but she couldn't summon up any enthusiasm to do so. Instead, she chose a gift from the box beside the table and selected paper covered with green holly and berries to wrap it. There was Christmas music playing softly in the background and steady traffic from the wrapping tables to the refreshment area. The mood was generally festive, with people chatting with their neighbors and friends while they worked.

Despite the activity all around her, Kayla was conscious of Trey's presence. Several times when her gaze slid across the room, she found him looking at her, and the heat in his eyes suggested that he was remembering the night they'd spent together.

She was remembering, too. Even before she'd learned that she was carrying his child—an undeniable reminder of that night—she hadn't been able to forget. She'd had only one cup of the spiked punch—or maybe it was two. Just enough to overcome her innate shyness and lessen her inhibitions, not enough to interfere with her memories of that night.

That evening had been the realization of a longtime fantasy. She'd had a secret crush on him all through high school, but she'd never let herself actually believe that he could want her, too. But for a few hours that night, she hadn't doubted for a moment that he did. The way he'd looked at her, the way he'd kissed her and touched her, had assured her that what was happening between them was mutual.

But the next day, he hadn't remembered any of it.

Or so she'd believed for five months.

Now she knew that he knew, but he was prepared to act as if nothing had ever happened. Unfortunately for Kayla, that wasn't really an option.

"Instead of staring at her from across the room, you could go over and talk to her."

Shane Roarke's suggestion forced Trey to tear his gaze away from Kayla. He pulled another piece of tape from the roll and resumed his wrapping.

"What?" he asked, as if he didn't know what—or rather whom—his friend was talking about.

Shane shook his head. "You're not fooling anyone, Trey."

"I don't know what you're talking about," he said.

But of course it was a lie. He'd noticed her the minute she'd walked through the door. He'd watched her come in, her nose and cheeks pink from the cold, and waited for her to come over and take the empty seat beside him. Her eyes had flicked in his direction, and his heart had pounded in anticipation. Then, much to his disappointment, she'd turned the other way.

"I'm talking about the pretty brunette across the room. The one with the big blue eyes and the shy smile who keeps looking over at you almost as much as you're looking at her."

"She's looking at me?"

Shane glanced at his wife and shook his head. "Was I ever this pathetic?"

"No," Gianna smiled indulgently. "You were worse."

Her husband chuckled. "I probably was," he acknowledged, reaching over to cover the hand that his wife had splayed over her enormous belly. "But look at us now."

Trey did look at them, and he was surprised by the little tug of envy he felt. He never thought he wanted what his friend had—certainly he wasn't looking to add a wife and a kid to his life just yet. But maybe, at some future time down the road.

For now, however, he couldn't stop thinking about Kayla. He'd told her that they could forget what happened between them on the Fourth of July, but it was a lie. He hadn't stopped thinking about her since that night, and now that he was back in Rust Creek Falls, he was eager to spend some time with her and to rekindle the chemistry that had sparked between them five months earlier.

"And look at his corners," Gianna said, interrupting his musing.

Trey followed her pointing finger to the package in front of him. "What's wrong with my corners?"

"They're lumpy."

"Shane's corners weren't so great, either, until you started helping him," he pointed out.

"That's true," Gianna agreed, pushing back her chair. She came around the table to his side. "Come on."

He eyed her warily. "Where are we going?"

"To get you some help."

He looked across the table at his friend and coworker; Shane just shrugged. Trey reluctantly rose to his feet and let Gianna lead him away. His steps faltered when he realized where she was leading, but she only grabbed his arm and tugged him along until they were standing by Kayla's table.

"You look like you know what you're doing," Gianna said to her. "Maybe you could help Trey with his wrapping?"

Kayla's pretty blue eyes shifted between them. "Help—how?"

"Show him how to fold the ends of the paper, for starters. He's making a mess of everything."

"You'd think a man who trains horses could handle a roll of paper," Kayla noted.

"You'd think," Gianna agreed. "But he can't."

"But I can hear," Trey pointed out. "And you're talking about me as if I'm not here."

"Sit," Gianna said, nudging him into a chair.

He sat.

"Good luck," she said to Kayla before she went back to her husband.

"I'm sorry about this," Trey said.

"About what?"

"Gianna dragging me over here."

"Why did she?"

He shrugged. "Partly because I was making a mess of everything. Mostly because I was paying more attention to you than my assigned task."

Her cheeks flushed prettily. "I'm sure you weren't making a mess of everything."

"You haven't seen me wrap anything yet," he warned her.

She handed him a box. "Give it a go."

He let his fingertips brush against hers in the exchange, and smiled when she drew away quickly. He laid the present on the paper and cut it to size, then wrapped the paper around the box. He was doing okay until he got to the ends, where he couldn't figure out how to fold it.

"You really do suck at this," she confirmed, amused by the fact.

"I'm not good with the paper," he admitted. "But I'm a tape master."

Her lips twitched, just a little, and her brows lifted. "A tape master?"

He demonstrated, tearing off four short, neat pieces of tape onto the tips of each of his fingers, and then transferring them one by one to secure the seams of the paper.

"Not too bad," she allowed.

"I have other talents," he told her.

"What kind of talents?"

He tipped his head closer to her and lowered his voice suggestively. "Why don't we go for a drive when we're finished here and…talk…about those talents?"

"I have a better idea," she said. "I'll cut and wrap, and you tape."

Her tone was prim but the pulse point at the base of her

jaw was racing. Satisfied by this proof that she wasn't as unaffected as she wanted him to believe, he backed off. "That'll work," he agreed. "For now."

The system of shared labor did work well, and they chatted while they wrapped. Their conversation was mostly easy and casual, but every once in a while, he'd allow his hand to brush against hers, or his knee to bump hers beneath the table. And every time they touched, her breath would catch and her gaze would slide away, reassuring him that the feelings churning inside him weren't entirely one-sided.

"I'm always impressed by the generosity of people at this time of year," he noted. "Even those folks who don't have a lot to give manage to make a contribution."

"You're right," Kayla agreed. "The year of the flood, when so many local families were struggling, Nina started the Tree of Hope to ensure that everyone in town had a holiday meal and presents under their tree. The response of the community was overwhelming."

"Nina Crawford?"

Kayla nodded. "Actually, she's Nina Traub now."

He'd grown up knowing about the feud between the Crawfords and the Traubs, although no one seemed to know for sure what had caused the rift between the families. Regardless of the origins, the animosity had endured through generations and escalated further when Nathan Crawford and Colin Traub both ran for the vacant mayoral seat after the flood. How Nathan's sister had ended up married to Colin's brother was a mystery to a lot of people, but their union showed promise of being the first step toward mending the rift between the families.

"The Tree of Hope is just one example of how the people of Rust Creek Falls look out for one another," she continued.

"I don't think I ever realized how much they did until I saw the way everyone pitched in and worked together after the flood."

"We had a lot of help from our Thunder Canyon neighbors, too," she reminded him. "And the money and publicity that Lissa brought in through Bootstraps was invaluable."

He nodded. "But looking around the town, I don't think anyone who wasn't here to see the devastation would ever guess how badly the town was hit."

"We're doing okay now."

"Better than okay, from what I've heard, since Maverick Manor opened its doors."

"Nate and Callie have big plans for their place, but I don't think the Thunder Canyon Resort needs to worry about its clientele heading this way."

"Have you ever been to the resort?" Trey asked.

She shook her head.

"You should come for a visit sometime."

Kayla wasn't sure if his statement was a general comment or an invitation, so she kept her response equally vague. "I've thought about it," she said. "In fact, I had considered doing some Christmas shopping that way."

"I wish you had come to Thunder Canyon," he said. "It would have been nice to spend some time with you without our every step being examined under the microscope of public opinion."

"Such is life in a small town," she said, glancing at the door to see Kristen and Ryan enter the hall.

"I didn't think you were going to make it," Kayla said to her sister.

"We didn't, either," Kristen admitted. "And I was exhausted after our final performance this week, but we both wanted to help out."

"There's no shortage of help," Trey said. "But still plenty

to do—especially if you have more wrapping experience than I do."

"How long have you guys been here?" Kristen asked.

"When I arrived, around seven-thirty, Trey was already here," Kayla told her.

"Which means you both must be ready for a break," Kristen decided. "Why don't Ryan and I take over for a little while so that you and Trey can take a walk to stretch your legs and get some fresh air?"

"Isn't it a little cold outside for an evening stroll?"

"Not if you bundle up," Kristen said.

Trey glanced from Kristen to her sister and back again. "Why do you want us to go for a walk?"

"Because Kayla needs to talk to you."

He looked at Kayla. "Can't we talk here?"

"No," Kristen said firmly, leaving her fiancé looking as confused as Trey felt. "Kayla needs to speak with you *privately*."

He looked at Kayla; she glared at her sister then offered him a halfhearted shrug.

"O-kay," he decided, pushing his chair away from the table.

Kayla did the same, sliding her arms into the sleeves of the ski jacket she'd draped over her chair.

It was frigid outside, and she shoved her hands into the pockets and tucked her chin into the collar of her jacket.

"It's going to snow," Trey said, pulling on his gloves.

"It's December in Montana," she agreed. "The odds are definitely in favor of more white stuff."

He chuckled at that. "So where are we walking to?"

"There's really nowhere to go."

"Then maybe you should just tell me why your sister was so determined to get us out of the community center so we could talk."

"Because she doesn't know how to mind her own business," Kayla grumbled.

But she knew her sister was right—Trey needed to know about the baby. And she needed to be the one to tell him.

"That's a little cryptic," he noted.

"I told you that Kristen knows what happened the night of the wedding," she reminded him.

He nodded.

"Well, she thought I should talk to you about…"

"About?" he prompted.

But her attention had been snagged by the approach of another couple. "I didn't know Forrest and Angie were in town."

Trey turned to follow the direction of her gaze. "They're very involved with Presents for Patriots."

Kayla wasn't surprised by this revelation. Forrest was one of six sons born to Bob and Ellie Traub but the only one who had opted for a career in the military rather than on the family ranch. Three years earlier, he'd returned from Iraq with a severely injured leg and PTSD. He'd gone to Thunder Canyon for treatment and therapy at the hospital there—although there was speculation that he'd wanted to escape all of the attention of being a hometown hero even more than he wanted to fix his leg. It was in Thunder Canyon that he'd met and fallen in love with Angie Anderson, and it warmed Kayla's heart to see how sincerely happy and content Forrest was now that he'd found the right woman to share his life.

They chatted with the war veteran and his wife for a few minutes before they continued into the hall. When the doors closed behind them, Kayla braced herself to speak once again. Then Bennett and Lucy Traub raced out of the community center, followed closely by their parents, Clay and Antonia.

"This isn't the easiest place to have a conversation, is it?" Trey asked when the Traubs had moved on.

"Not tonight," she agreed.

"So maybe we should try something different," he suggested, and lowered his head to touch his mouth to hers.

He caught her off guard.

Kayla had been so preoccupied thinking about the conversation they weren't having that she didn't realize his intention until he was kissing her. And then her brain shut down completely as her body melted against his.

Trey wrapped his arms around her, holding her as close as their bulky outerwear would allow. She lifted her arms to link them behind his head, holding on to him as the world spun beneath her feet.

It was funny—they couldn't seem to have a two-minute conversation without being interrupted, but the kiss they shared went on and on, blissfully, endlessly. When Trey finally eased his lips from hers, they were both breathless.

"I wondered," he said.

"What did you wonder?"

"If your lips would taste as I remembered."

"Do they?"

"No," he said. "They taste even better."

She felt her cheeks flush despite the chilly air. "I thought you wanted to forget about that night."

"I'm not sorry about what happened between us in the summer. I just wish we hadn't rushed into bed."

"I'd guess that had more to do with the punch than either of us," she said.

"Or the chemistry between us."

"I thought the alcohol was responsible for the chemistry."

"Have you been drinking tonight?"

She flushed. "Of course not."

"Because from where I'm standing, that kiss we just shared proves the sparks between us are real, and I'd like to spend some time with you while I'm in town over the holidays, so that we can get to know one another better, and maybe see where the chemistry leads us."

"But you're only going to be in town for a few weeks," she reminded him—reminded both of them.

"Thunder Canyon isn't that far away."

"And I'm sure there's no shortage of women there."

"There's not," he agreed. "But I haven't stopped thinking about you since July. I haven't been out with another woman in all that time because I didn't want to go out with anyone else."

His words stirred hope in her heart. If he really meant what he was saying, maybe they could build a relationship—except that anything they started to build now would be on a foundation of lies, or at least omission.

Her baby—their baby—kicked inside her belly, a not-so-subtle reminder of that omission.

"Trey…"

"Just give us a chance," he urged.

"I want to," she admitted. "But—"

He touched his fingers to her lips. "It's enough that you're willing to give us a chance."

She shook her head. "There are things you don't know. Things you need to know."

"We've got time to find out everything we need to know about one another," he told her. "I don't want to rush anything."

And she let herself be persuaded, because it was easier than telling him the truth.

Or so she thought until she considered having to go back inside and face her sister. Because she knew Kristen would take one look at her and immediately know that she'd failed in her assigned task.

"We should probably get back inside before people start whispering and my grandparents read about our disappearance from the gift-wrapping in Rust Creek Ramblings."

"They won't read anything in the paper," she told him.

His brows lifted. "How can you be so certain?"

Kayla wasn't quite sure how to respond to that.

"Is that what your sister wanted you to tell me?"

"What?"

"That you're the Rust Creek Rambler."

She gasped, shocked as much by his casual delivery as the statement itself. "Why would you think that?"

"The first clue was your assurance that Kristen wasn't the Rust Creek Rambler. It occurred to me that the only way you could be so certain was if you knew the true identity of the Rambler. And then, when we saw Will and Jordyn Leigh at the diner, you made reference to their *intoxicated nuptials*—which was, coincidentally, the same phrase that was used in the 'Ramblings' column."

She was surprised that he'd figured it out. She'd been writing the column for three and a half years with no one, aside from the paper's editor, being aware of her identity.

"You're right," she admitted softly. "But no one else in town has ever shown any suspicion about me being the author of the column."

"Maybe because no one else has been paying close attention to you."

"Are you mad?"

"Why would I be mad?"

"Because I kept it from you."

"And everyone else in town."

She nodded.

"Actually, I'm more baffled—especially when I think

about what was written in Ramblings about the two of us dancing together at the wedding."

She shrugged. "Several people saw us together. If I'd ignored that, it would have been suspicious. By mentioning it in the column, it deflected attention away from me as the possible author."

"Clever," he noted. "So tell me, is your copy editing job real or just a cover?"

"It's real, but only part of what I do."

"You are full of surprises," he told her. "But I'm not sure why it mattered so much to your sister that you tell me about your secret occupation."

"Kristen's a big fan of open communication," she told him. "But I wouldn't be able to do my job if everyone knew that I was the Rambler, so I'd appreciate it if you didn't out me to the whole community."

"I think, if I'm going to keep such a big secret for you, I'm going to need something in return."

"What kind of something?" she asked warily.

"Help with my Christmas shopping?" he suggested.

She smiled. "You've got a deal."

Kayla hadn't seen Trey since their gift-wrapping at the community center. She'd been lying low on purpose—not just because she still hadn't figured out how to tell him about the baby, but because she wanted to be able to tell her sister that she hadn't seen him and, therefore, hadn't had a chance to tell him.

Apparently, she was a liar *and* a coward. And while she wasn't particularly proud of her behavior, she consoled herself with the assurance that these were desperate times.

Thursday afternoon she went into the newspaper office again to work on the Sunday edition of the paper and polish her own column. Unfortunately, the onset of winter meant that many residents were hunkered down indoors rather than creating and disseminating juicy headlines.

There were rumors that Alistair Warren had spent several hours with the widow next door during a recent storm—"much longer than it would take to fill her firebox with wood" she'd heard from one source—but Kayla didn't have much more than that for her column.

She considered mentioning that Trey Strickland had recently been spotted at Crawford's buying diapers, but putting his name into any context with babies hit a little too close to the secret she was keeping—and knew she couldn't continue to keep for much longer.

Already her mother was looking at her with that calculating gleam in her eye, as if she knew her daughter was hiding something from her. Kayla's father—always preoccupied with ranch business—probably wouldn't notice if she sat down at the breakfast table with a ring through her nose, but her mother had always had an uncanny sense when it came to every one of her five children.

Kayla wanted to share the news of her baby with her family. She wasn't particularly proud of the circumstances surrounding the conception, but she wasn't ashamed of her baby. And the further she progressed in her pregnancy, the more she wanted to talk to her mother about being a mother, about the changes her body was going through and the confusing array of emotions she was experiencing. She wanted to share her thoughts and feelings with someone who had been through what she was going through right now.

Kristen had been great—aside from the constant pressure to tell Trey—but her sister was so caught up in the excitement of being in love and planning her wedding, she couldn't imagine the doubts and fears that overwhelmed Kayla.

She so desperately wanted to do right by her baby, to give her child the life he or she deserved. Of course, Kristen kept insisting the baby was a he, despite the fact that the ultrasound photo gave nothing away.

Kayla opened the zippered pocket inside her purse and carefully removed that photo now. At the time it was taken, her baby had measured about five inches long and weighed around seven ounces.

"About the size of a bell pepper," the technician had said, to help Kayla put the numbers into perspective.

She'd also reassured the mother-to-be that baby had all the requisite parts—although the baby's positioning didn't reveal whether there were boy parts or girl parts—but it was the rapid beating of the tiny heart on the monitor that snagged Kayla's attention and filled her own heart.

She'd marveled at the baby's movements on the screen, but she hadn't been able to feel any of those movements inside her. Not until almost three weeks later.

She was much more attuned to the tiny flutters and kicks now. Of course, the baby seemed most active when she was trying to sleep at night, but she didn't mind. Alone in her room, she would put her hands on her belly and let herself think about the tiny person growing inside her.

Her doctor had suggested that she start looking into childbirth classes. Kayla understood the wisdom of this advice, but she didn't dare register for classes in Rust Creek Falls and she didn't know that she'd be able to get to Kalispell every week to commit to classes there. Although Kalispell was a much bigger city than Rust Creek Falls, her encounter with Melba Strickland at the shopping mall had reminded her that she couldn't count on anonymity there. Instead, she'd been reading everything she could find and had even been taking online classes about pregnancy and childbirth.

As she traced the outline of her baby's shape with her fingertip, she hoped her efforts were enough. She was so afraid of doing something wrong, of somehow screwing up this tiny, fragile life that was growing inside her.

She wanted to show the picture to Trey; she wanted to talk about her hopes and dreams for their child and share her fears. Mostly, she wanted him to want to be part of their child's life, because she didn't want to raise their child alone. She wanted her baby to have two parents.

The beep of her phone interrupted her thoughts. She carefully tucked the photo away again before checking the message from her sister.

I want it!

She opened the attachment to see what *it* was, and smiled at the picture of a multi-tiered wedding cake. Each stacked layer was elaborately decorated with a different white-on-white design: silhouettes of bucking broncos, cowboy boots, cowboy hats and horseshoes.

Despite the Western motif, it was elegant and unique— totally Kristen.

She texted back,

Luv it

Because she did. She didn't have a clue where her sister would find someone in their small town capable of re-creating such a work of art, but that was a practical worry for another day. Right now her sister was dreaming of her perfect day, and Kayla was happy to be drawn into the fantasy with her.

Kristen had asked Kayla to be her maid of honor, and she had, of course, accepted, but she needed to talk to her twin about the timing of the event and the likelihood that she would be a maid of *dis*honor. She didn't think Kristen would want to be upstaged on her wedding day by her hugely pregnant and unwed sister. As much as Kristen enjoyed the spotlight, Kayla didn't think she'd want the happiest day of her life tainted by that kind of scandal.

Upon receiving her reply, Kristen immediately called. "Are you sick and tired of hearing about the wedding?" she asked.

"Never," Kayla assured her sister.

"Then you won't mind if Mom and I drag you into Kalispell tomorrow to go shopping for my dress?"

"Are you kidding? I've been wondering when you'd finally get around to that." She knew that Ryan had offered to fly his fiancée out to California so that she could shop on Rodeo Drive in Beverly Hills, but the idea hadn't appealed to Kristen. Her twin was surprisingly traditional in a lot of ways—and very much a country girl.

"I've just been so busy with the play that I haven't had much free time," Kristen said now. "But June isn't that far away, so I figured I'd better make time to start preparing for the wedding."

"You've set a date, then?"

"June eleventh," her sister confirmed.

"Then I guess we'd better find you a dress."

Chapter Seven

When Trey saw Kayla's truck pull up in front of the boarding house, for a moment he thought—hoped—she had come into town to see him. When he saw her lift a small box out of the passenger seat of her vehicle, he was disappointed to realize she had another reason for being there.

He met her at the door and took the box from her. "What's this?"

"Your grandmother wanted a couple of jars of bread-and-butter pickles."

"She makes her own pickles."

Kayla shrugged. "Apparently, your grandfather was looking for something in the cellar and knocked over a shelf and she lost the last of hers."

He hadn't heard anything about such an incident—and he was pretty sure if his grandfather had truly engineered such a mishap, the whole town would have heard about it. More likely his grandmother had engineered the story to bring Kayla to the boarding house, and though he didn't approve of Melba's meddling, he wouldn't complain about the results.

"Did she happen to mention why she needed—" he glanced into the box "—half a dozen jars of pickles right now, today?"

"She spoke to my mother, not me. I'm just the delivery girl."

"Because I'm sure you didn't have anything better to do," he said dryly.

"Not according to my mother," she agreed.

"Do you have anything else on your schedule today?"

"No, but I figured, since I was coming into town, I would stop in at the newspaper office and try to get a head start on editing anything that has been submitted for the next edition."

"Or you could help me," he suggested.

"Help you with what?" she asked, a little warily.

"I've been tasked with finding the perfect Christmas tree for the main floor parlor."

"Perfect is a matter of interpretation when it comes to Christmas trees," she warned him.

"I figure as long as it's approximately the right height and shape, it's perfect."

Kayla *tsked* as she shook her head. "What kind of tree does your grandmother want?"

"A green one."

She laughed. "Well, that narrows your search to most of Montana."

He shrugged. "She didn't seem concerned about specifics so much as timing—it's only two weeks before Christmas, and she wants a tree in the parlor today."

"Where in the parlor?" Kayla pressed. "Does she want something slender that can be tucked into a corner? Or would she prefer a fuller shape that will become the centerpiece of the room?"

It was an effort to refrain from rolling his eyes. "I don't know. I just know that the tree is always in the corner—with stacks of presents piled underneath it on Christmas morning."

She smiled. "Everyone's a kid at Christmas, aren't they?"

"You don't get excited about presents?"

"Of course I do."

"So will you help me out with the tree?"

She pulled back the cuff of her jacket to look at the watch on her wrist. "Sure."

Twenty minutes later he pulled into the parking lot of a tree farm on the edge of town.

"I didn't expect it would be this busy in the middle of the day on a weekday," he commented.

"Two weeks," she reminded him.

However, most of the customers seemed to be examining precut trees, and although he knew that was the easier option, his grandmother had specifically requested a fresh-cut tree and had sent her husband out to the shed to get the bow saw for him.

They walked down the path, following the signs toward the "cut your own" section of the farm.

"Aside from green, what should I be looking for?" Trey asked Kayla.

"It depends on what matters most to you—scent, color, hardiness. Balsam fir smells lovely but they tend to be bulky around the bottom and take up a lot of space. The Scotch pine is probably the most common type of Christmas tree. Its bright green color is appealing, but the branches and needles tend to be quite stiff, making it more difficult—and painful—to decorate."

"You're not a fan," he guessed.

"They're pretty trees," she insisted. "But no, they wouldn't be my first choice."

"How do you know so much about Christmas trees?"

She shrugged. "Every year, from as far back as I can remember, we've trekked deep into the woods to cut down a tree, so I probably could have steered you in the right direction on the basis of that experience without necessarily knowing what was a spruce or a fir. The technical stuff I learned when I edited an article—'Choosing the Perfect Christmas Tree'—for the newspaper a couple of years back."

"You must get to read some interesting stuff in your job."

"I do," she agreed. "And not just in the "Ramblings" column."

"That doesn't count, anyway—you make that stuff up."

"I do not," she said indignantly. "I simply report facts that are brought to my attention."

"There's a fair amount of speculation in addition to the facts," he noted.

"Speculation about the facts, perhaps," she allowed.

He shook his head, but he was smiling when he paused beside a blue spruce. "What do you think of this one?"

She let her gaze run up the tall—extremely tall, in fact—trunk. "I think it's a beautiful tree for the town square but way too big for anyone's parlor."

He nodded in acknowledgment. "Who picks out the tree in your family?"

"Majority rules, but there's usually a lot of arguing before a final decision is made. My mom has a tendency to pick out a bigger tree than we have room for, which means my dad ends up muttering and cursing as he cuts down the trunk 'just another inch more' or trims some of the branches 'just on one side' so it'll end up sitting closer to the wall." She smiled a little at the memory. "My dad now carries a tape measure, so that he can show my mother that a tree isn't 'perfect' for an eight-foot room when it's actually eleven feet tall."

"I suspect my grandmother has had the opposite experience, because she made a point of telling me that the room has a twelve-foot ceiling and she doesn't want anything shorter than ten feet, preferably ten and a half."

"Did you bring a tape measure?"

He pulled it out of his pocket to show her.

"Did you bring a ladder so that you can measure up to ten feet?"

"It's in my other pocket."

She laughed.

He looked at her—at her cheeks pink from the cold, at the delicate white flakes of snow against her dark hair and at her eyes, as clear and blue as the sky, sparkling in the sun—and realized that he was in danger of falling hard and fast.

And in that moment, he didn't care.

He caught her hand, halting her in midstride. She tipped her head back to look up at him, and he lowered his head to touch his mouth to hers.

He kissed her softly, savoring the moment. He loved kissing her, loved the way her lips yielded and her body melted. He loved the quiet sounds she made deep in her throat.

But he wanted more than a few stolen kisses. He wanted to make love with her again, to enjoy not just the taste of her lips but the joining of their bodies. But he'd promised that they could take things slow this time, and he intended to keep that promise—even if it meant yet another cold shower when he got back to the boarding house.

When he finally eased his lips away, she looked as dazed as he felt. "What was that for?"

"Does there need to be a reason for me to kiss you?"

"I guess not," she admitted. "You just…surprised me."

He smiled at that. "You surprise me every time I see you."

"I do?"

"You do," he confirmed. "I always thought I knew you. You were Derek's sister, the shy twin, the quiet one. But I've realized there's a lot more to you than most people give you credit for."

"I am the shy twin, the quiet one."

He slid his arms around her, wanting to draw her nearer. "You're also smart and beautiful and passionate."

She put her hands on his chest, her arms locked to hold him at a distance. "Tree," she reminded him.

"They're not going anywhere," he noted.

"You say that now, but do you see that stump there?"

He followed the direction of her gaze. "Yeah."

"That might have been *your* perfect tree, but someone else got to it before you did."

"So I'll find another perfect tree."

"Do you think it will be that easy? That perfect trees just—"

"Grow like trees," he interjected drily.

Her lips curved. "Touché."

Half an hour later, they were headed back to the boarding house with a lovely tree tied down in the box of Trey's truck.

When they arrived, they found that Gene had carted out all of the decorations: lights and garland and ornaments.

"Looks like our work isn't done yet," he noted.

"I thought your grandmother usually let her guests help with the trimming of the tree."

"Apparently she stopped that a couple of years ago, when a three-year-old decided to throw some of her favorite ornaments rather than hang them. A few of them were mouth-blown glass that a cousin had brought back for her from Italy."

Kayla winced sympathetically.

"She has a story for every ornament on her tree," Trey told her. "And now a story for eight that aren't."

She tucked her hands behind her back. "Now I'm afraid to touch anything."

"You can touch me," Trey told her, with a suggestive wink. "I won't break."

Kayla laughed. "Let's focus on the tree," she responded, stepping out of his reach.

But Trey circled around the tree in the other direction and caught her against him. "Now I have to kiss you."

"Have to?" She lifted a brow. "Why?"

"Because you're standing under the mistletoe."

Kayla looked up, but there was no mistletoe hanging from the ceiling above her. There was, however, a sprig of the recognizable plant in Trey's hand, which he was holding above her head.

"That's cheating," she told him.

"I don't care," he said and touched his mouth to hers.

As Kayla melted into the kiss, her objections melted away.

The slamming of the back door returned her to her senses. "It's only two weeks until Christmas," she reminded him. "And your grandmother wants her tree up."

He sighed regretfully but released her so they could focus on the assigned task.

After leaving the boarding house, Kayla stopped at Crawford's to pick up a quart of milk for her mother. She was carrying the jug to the checkout counter when she saw Tara Jones, a third-grade teacher from the local elementary school.

"This is a lucky coincidence," the teacher said.

"Why's that?" she asked curiously.

"Our annual holiday pageant is in less than a week and we're way behind schedule with the costumes and scenery. I know it's a huge imposition," Tara said, "but we could really use your help."

"It's not an imposition at all," Kayla told her. "I'd be happy to pitch in."

"Thank you, thank you, thank you. We do have other volunteers who can assist you, but I think one of the biggest problems is that no one was willing to take the lead because they're not sure what they should be doing. But with your experience in the Kalispell theater, you should have them on track in no time."

"When do you need me?"

"Yesterday."

Kayla laughed.

"Okay, Monday would work," Tara relented. "Three o'clock?"

"I'll be there."

"And if you want to bring your beau, I'm sure no one would have any objections to an extra pair of hands."

She frowned. "What?"

"Come on, Kayla. Do you really think people haven't noticed that you've been spending a lot of time with Trey Strickland?"

"I wouldn't say it's a lot of time," she hedged.

"So you're not exclusive?"

She frowned at the question. "We're not even really dating—just hanging out together."

"Is that what you told the Rambler?"

"What?"

The other woman shrugged. "I just wondered how it is that everyone knows you and Trey have been hanging out, but that little tidbit has yet to make the gossip column of the local paper."

"Probably because it's not newsworthy."

"That's one theory," Tara agreed. "Another is that the Rambler is someone you know."

"Or maybe it's someone Trey knows," she countered.

"I guess that is another possibility. But you can bet if I was dating Trey Strickland, I'd shout it out from the headlines."

Trey was shoveling the walk that led to the steps of the boarding house when he heard someone say, "Hey, stranger."

He recognized his friend's voice before he turned and came face-to-face with Derek Dalton. The instinctive pleasure was quickly supplanted by guilt. Derek had been his best friend in high school and one of the first people he sought out whenever he returned to Rust Creek Falls, but he hadn't done so this time because he didn't know how to see Derek without feeling guilty about what had happened with Derek's sister. And now he had another reason to feel guilty, because he was dating Kayla behind her brother's back.

"What brings you into town?" Trey asked.

"I'm heading over to the Ace in the Hole for a beer and thought I'd see if you wanted to join me."

Trey had decided to tackle the shoveling while he waited for Kayla to respond to any of the three messages he'd left for her. Since that had yet to happen, he decided he'd look pretty pathetic sitting at home waiting for her to call.

"Let me finish up here and grab a quick shower," Trey said.

While he was doing that, Derek visited with Melba and

Gene, hanging out in their kitchen as he'd often done when he and Trey were teenagers.

Trey was quick in the shower, then he checked for messages on his phone again. *Nada.*

He pushed Kayla from his mind and headed out with her brother.

They climbed the rough-hewn wooden steps and opened the screen door beneath the oversize playing card—an ace of hearts—that blinked in neon red. Inside, a long wooden bar ran the length of one wall with a dozen bar stools facing the mirrored wall that reflected rows of glass bottles. Shania Twain was singing from the ancient Wurlitzer jukebox at the back of the room.

There was a small and rarely used dance floor in the middle of the room, surrounded by scarred wooden tables and ladder-back chairs. The floor was littered with peanut shells that crunched under their boots as they made their way to the bar, taking the last two empty stools. He nodded to Alex Monroe, foreman of the local lumber mill, who lifted his beer in acknowledgment.

Trey settled onto his stool and looked around. "This place hasn't changed at all, has it?"

"Isn't that part of its charm?"

"It has charm?"

Derek chuckled. "Don't let Rosey hear you say that."

"She still in charge of this place?"

"Claims it's the only relationship that ever worked out for her."

"Sounds like Rosey," Trey agreed.

The bartender delivered their drinks and they settled back, falling into familiar conversation about ranching and horses and life in Rust Creek Falls. They were on their second round of drinks when two girls in tight jeans and low-cut shirts squeezed up to the bar beside them on the pretext of wanting to order, but the flirtatious glances they sent toward Trey and Derek suggested they were looking for more than drinks.

The girls accepted their beverages from the bartender then headed toward an empty table, inviting Trey and Derek to join them.

"What do you say?" Derek asked, his gaze riveted on their swaying hips as the girls walked away.

Trey shook his head, not the least bit tempted.

"C'mon, buddy. You're supposed to be my wing man."

"Don't you ever get tired of women throwing themselves at you?"

Derek laughed. "That's funny."

Trey frowned.

"You weren't joking?"

"No," he said.

"You meet someone?"

"As a matter of fact, I did."

Derek obviously hadn't expected an affirmative response, but he shrugged it off, anyway. "So even if you've got a girl in Thunder Canyon, she wouldn't ever know about a meaningless hookup here."

He didn't correct his friend's assumption that he was seeing someone in Thunder Canyon. If he admitted that he was interested in a local girl, Derek would be full of questions—questions that Trey wasn't prepared to answer. So all he said was, "*I'd* know."

Derek shook his head. "She's really got her hooks into you, doesn't she?"

Trey frowned at the phrasing, but he'd recently started to admit—at least to himself—that it was probably true. "Your turn will come someday," he warned his friend.

"Maybe," Derek allowed, setting his empty bottle on the bar. "But that day is not today."

"Where are you going?" he demanded when Kayla's brother slid off his stool.

"When a girl gives me a 'come hither' glance, I come hither."

Trey just shook his head as he watched him walk away to join the two girls at the table they now occupied.

Even if Kayla did have her hooks in him, so to speak, he knew there were still obstacles to a relationship between them, and the geographical distance between Thunder Canyon and Rust Creek Falls was one of the biggest.

But that distance wasn't an issue right now, and he really wanted to see her. He slipped his phone out of his pocket and checked for messages. There were none.

He scrolled through his list of contacts, clicked on her name then the message icon. The blank white screen seemed blindingly bright in the dimly lit bar.

Just thinking abt u, wondering what u r doing…

There was no immediate reply. Of course not—whatever she was doing, she obviously wasn't sitting around waiting to hear from him.

He glanced over at the girls' table, where his friend was holding another bottle of beer. Derek caught his eye and waved him over, but Trey shook his head again. Then he tossed some money on the bar to pay for his drink and walked back to the boarding house.

Kayla didn't get Trey's message until the morning, and her heart fluttered inside her chest when she picked up her phone and saw his name on the screen. She clicked on the message icon.

Just thinking abt u, wondering what u r doing…

The time stamp indicated that he'd reached out to her at 10:28 pm.

Sorry—I was in the barn all night watching over a new litter of kittens.

He replied immediately.

Everything okay?

8 kittens, only 5 survived.

Tough night for you.

She hadn't expected his immediate and unquestioning understanding. It had been a tough night. Yeah, she'd grown up on a ranch and seen a lot of births and deaths, but it still hurt to lose an animal. She'd tried to keep the kittens warm with blankets and hot water bottles and her own body heat, but the three she'd lost had just been too small.

I'm sorry I didn't have a chance to call.

Me 2. I ended up @ the Ace with Derek.

She had enough secrets in her life, but she wasn't ready for the third degree from her family when they learned that she'd been hanging out with Trey Strickland, because they all knew that she'd had a huge crush on her brother's best friend in high school. And though she wasn't proud of her instinctive cringe, she had to ask.

You didn't say anything about us?

There r enough brawls there without giving your brother an excuse to hit me.

She exhaled a sigh of relief.

Good. I like your nose where it is.

Me 2. But now I'm wondering…r u ashamed of our relationship?

I'm just not sure what our relationship is.

Maybe we can work on figuring it out today.

Which was an undeniably tempting offer. She missed him more than she wanted to admit, conscious with each day that passed that he wasn't going to be in Rust Creek Falls for very long, and the time was quickly slipping away. Unfortunately, she knew that they wouldn't be able to figure out anything that day.

I'm on maid of honor duty today—looking for Kristen's wedding dress.

All day?

Knowing my sister, probably.

OK. I'll touch base with u 2morrow.

I'm at the theater 2morrow. But I'm free Tuesday.

Tuesday is too far away.

It was far away, and the fact that he thought so, too, put a smile on her face as she got ready to go shopping with the bride-to-be.

RUST CREEK RAMBLINGS: DECK THE COWBOY
Local cowboys have been showing their holiday spirit...or maybe it would be more accurate to say that Tommy Wheeler and Jared Winfree demonstrated the effect of imbibing *too many* holiday spirits after the men went a couple of rounds at the Ace in the Hole this past Friday night! Both were declared winners in the brawl and awarded a free night's accommodation in the sheriff's lockup as well as receiving a detailed bill for damages from everyone's favorite bar owner, Rosey Travern.

Chapter Eight

Kristen tried on at least a dozen different styles of wedding dresses—from long sleeves to strapless, slim-fitting to hoop skirts, simple taffeta to all-over lace decorated with tiny beads and crystals. And she looked stunning in each and every one. Even the layers and layers of ruffled organza that would have looked like an explosion of cotton candy on anyone else looked wonderful on Kristen.

"You must at least have a particular style in mind," Rita Dalton chided, when Kristen went back to the sample rack and selected four more completely different dresses again.

"I don't," the bride-to-be insisted. "But I think I'll know it when I see it."

But none of those four dresses seemed to be the right one, either. Rita moved away from the bridal gowns to peruse a more colorful rack of dresses.

"What do you think of this for your maid of honor?" she asked, lifting a hanger from the bar.

"Oh, I *love* the color," Kristen agreed, touching a hand

to the cornflower taffeta. "The blue is almost a perfect match to Kayla's eyes."

Kayla glanced at the dress. "It is pretty."

"You should try it on," Rita urged.

Her panicked gaze flew to her sister. Though Kristen understood the cause of her panic, she was at a loss to help her out of the sticky situation.

Rita looked at the tag. "This is a size six—perfect."

The dress wasn't only a size six, it was also very fitted, and there was no way Kayla could squeeze into the sample without revealing her baby bump.

"Today is about finding Kristen a dress," she reminded their mother.

"But if Kristen likes it and you like it, why can't we pick out your dress, too?"

"Because the bridesmaids' dresses should complement the bride's style—which means that there's no point in considering any options until she's chosen her dress."

"But look at this," Kristen said, coming to her rescue by holding up another outfit. "Doesn't it just scream 'mother-of-the-bride'?"

Rita glanced over, the irritated frown on her brow smoothing out when she saw the elegant sheath-style dress with bolero jacket that Kristen was holding.

Thank you, Kayla mouthed to her sister behind their mother's back.

"I'm not sure I want a dress that screams anything," Rita said. "But that is lovely."

Kristen shoved the dress into their mother's hands and steered her into the fitting room she'd recently vacated. They left the store thirty minutes later with a dress for the mother-of-the-bride but nothing for the bride herself.

"There's another bridal shop just down the street," Rita said.

"Can we go for lunch first?" Kristen asked. "I'm starving."

"Priorities," their mother chided. "June is only six months away, and you need a gown."

"I need to eat or I'm going to pass out in a puddle of taffeta."

Rita glanced at her watch. "All right—we'll go for a quick bite."

They found a familiar chain restaurant not too far away. Even before she looked at the menu, Kayla's mouth was watering for French fries and gravy, a lunchtime staple from high school that she hadn't craved in recent years—until she got pregnant. After a brief perusal of the menu, she set it aside.

"What are you having?" Kristen asked.

"The chicken club wrap and fries."

Her mother frowned. "French fries, Kayla?"

"What's wrong with French fries?" she asked, aware that she sounded more than a little defensive.

"Do you think I don't know the real reason you didn't want to try on that dress is that you're afraid you won't fit into a size six right now?"

"I've put on a few pounds," she admitted. "Not twenty." At least, not yet.

"It always starts with a few," her mother said, not unsympathetically.

"What starts with a few?"

"Emotional eating."

Kayla looked at Kristen, to see if her sister was having better luck following their mother's logic, but Kristen just shrugged.

"I understand that it's hard," Rita continued.

"What's hard?"

She glanced across the table at her other daughter. "You

and Kristen have always been close. You've always done so many things together. Now your sister is getting married, and you're afraid that you're going to be alone."

She opened her mouth to protest then decided that if that was the excuse her mother was willing to believe, why would she dissuade her?

"I'm going to wash up," Rita said. "If the server comes before I'm back, you can order the chicken Caesar for me."

"And people think I'm the only actress in the family," Kristen commented when their mother had gone.

"Am I really that pathetic?" Kayla wanted to know. "Do you think I'd ever be so devastated over the lack of a man in my life that I'd eat myself into a bigger dress size?"

"You're not pathetic at all," her sister said loyally. "And if Mom had seen you and Trey dancing at the wedding, she'd realize how far off base she is. Then again, if she'd seen you two dancing at the wedding, she might suspect the real reason you're craving French fries."

"She's right about the weight gain, though," Kayla admitted. "I'm up nine pounds already."

"And still wearing your skinny jeans." She lifted the hem of her sweater to show that the button was unfastened and the zipper half-undone.

"Wow—we're going to have to paint 'Goodyear' on you and float you up in the sky pretty soon."

"Sure, you're making jokes," Kayla said. "But at dinner Sunday night, when I said that yes, I would like some dessert, Mom cut me a sliver of lemon meringue pie that was so narrow, I could see through the filling."

"So tell her that you're pregnant," her sister advised. "I bet she'd let you have seconds of dessert if she knew you were eating for two."

"If she didn't drown the pie with her tears of disappointment and shame first. And then, of course, she'd demand to know who the father is—"

"And daddy would get out his shotgun," Kristen interjected.

She shook her head. "Definitely not a good scene."

"But probably inevitable," her sister said. "Which is why you have to tell Trey."

Kayla sighed. "I know."

The server came and they ordered their lunches—Kayla opting for a side salad rather than fries to appease her mother. Kristen chose the same sandwich as her sister but with the fries and gravy that Kayla wanted.

"When are you seeing Trey again?" Kristen asked when the waiter left them alone again.

"I don't know."

"You need to make a plan to see him," her sister insisted. "And you need to *tell him*."

"Tell who what?" Rita asked, returning to her seat at the table.

"I need to, uh, tell Derek that Midnight Shadow was favoring her right foreleg when I moved her out of her stall this morning."

"He won't be happy about that," their mother noted.

"Hopefully it isn't anything serious," Kristen said.

When their meals were delivered, talk shifted back to the wedding. Kayla ate her salad, silently promising the baby that she'd have something fatty and salty later, when she'd escaped from the eagle eye of her mother.

"What did you think of the dresses I tried on?" Kristen asked her sister, as she dragged a thick fry through the puddle of gravy on her plate. "And I want your honest opinion."

Kayla focused on her own plate and stabbed a cherry tomato with her fork. "I think they were all beautiful dresses and you looked stunning in each one."

"That's not very helpful," Kristen chided.

"Well, it's true. It's also true that I don't think any of them was the right dress for you."

"Why not?"

She chewed the tomato. "Because they were all too... designer."

Kristen wrinkled her nose. "What does that even mean?"

"It means that you're trying too hard to look like a Hollywood bride."

"Ryan lived and worked in Hollywood for a lot of years, surrounded by some of the world's most beautiful women," her sister pointed out. "I don't want to disappoint him on our wedding day."

"Think about what you just said," Kayla told her. "Yes, your fiancé was surrounded by beautiful women in Hollywood—but he didn't fall in love until he came to Montana and met *you*. So why would you want to be anything different than the woman he fell in love with?"

"I don't," Kristen said.

"Remember the first dress you looked at—the one you instinctively gravitated toward and then put back on the rack without trying it on because it was too simple?"

"The one with the little cap sleeves and the open back?"

Kayla nodded. "You need to go back and try it on."

"I will," Kristen decided, popping another French fry into her mouth. "Right after we finish lunch."

"How was shopping with your sister and your mother?" Trey asked Kayla, when he called the next morning.

She let out a deep sigh. "It was...an experience."

"Did Kristen find a dress?"

"I think it was about the thirty-fifth one she tried on, but yes, she finally found it."

"Does that mean you're free today?"

"It means I don't have to go shopping," she told him. "But I do have to bake Christmas cookies."

"Okay, what are you doing after that?"

"I'm probably going to be tied up in the kitchen most of the day," she told him.

He paused. "I was really hoping we could spend some time together."

She was hoping for the same thing, especially since she knew that Trey's time in Rust Creek Falls was limited. "Do you want to come over and help me make cookies?"

"I can't believe I'm actually saying this," he noted. "But yes, if that's the only way I can be with you, I do."

"You know where to find me."

"Will I find coffee there, too?"

"There will definitely be coffee," she assured him.

It wasn't until he pulled into the long drive of the Circle D Ranch that he considered the possible awkwardness of the situation if Derek was at the main house. Not that his friend's potential disapproval would have affected his decision to come, but he should have factored him into the equation and he hadn't. He hadn't thought about anything but how much he wanted to see Kayla.

When he got to the house, there was no sign of Derek—or anyone else other than Kayla. "Where is everyone?"

"My parents went to an equipment auction in Missoula, and my brothers are out doing whatever they do around the ranch."

"So no one will interrupt if I kiss you?"

"No one will interrupt," she promised.

He dipped his head toward her. "Mmm...you smell really good."

She laughed softly. "I think it's the cookies."

He nuzzled her throat, making her blood heat and her knees quiver. "No, it's definitely you."

"You smell good, too." She kissed him lightly. "And taste even better."

He drew her closer, kissed her longer and deeper—until the oven timer began to buzz.

Saved by the bell, Kayla thought, embarrassed to realize that she'd momentarily forgotten they were standing in the middle of her mother's kitchen, making out like teenagers.

"You said no one would interrupt," he reminded her.

"Mechanical timers excluded." She moved away from him to slide her hand into an oven mitt and take the pan out of the oven.

While she was doing that, he surveyed the ingredients, bowls and utensils spread out over the counter. "How many cookies do you plan to make?"

She gestured toward the counter. "The list is there."

He read aloud: "Pecan Sandies, Coconut Macaroons, Brownies, Peppermint Fudge, Sugar Cookies, Rocky Road Squares, Snowballs, Peanut Brittle, White Chocolate Chip Cookies with Macadamia Nuts and Dried Cherries." He glanced up. "You don't have a shorter name for that one?"

She shook her head.

"Well, I guess people would at least know what they're getting," he acknowledged. "As opposed to a snowball."

"Snowballs are one of my favorites," she told him. "Chopped dates, nuts and crispy rice cereal rolled in coconut."

"There's no gingerbread on the list."

"Kristen and I baked that last week."

"What are these?" he asked, pointing to a plate of cookies she'd baked earlier.

"Those are the Pecan Sandies."

"Can I try one?"

"Sure," she said.

He bit into the flaky pastry. "Mmm. This is good," he mumbled around a mouthful of cookie. "No wonder so many people put on weight over the holidays with these kinds of goodies to sample."

She froze with the spatula in hand, wondering if he was just making a casual comment or if he'd noticed the extra pounds she was carrying. She was wearing yoga pants and a shapeless top that disguised all of her curves, but especially the one of her belly.

"What can I do to help?" Trey asked. "Because if you don't give me a job, I'll just eat everything you make."

She chided herself for being paranoid and turned her attention back to the task at hand. "You can start by pouring yourself a cup of the coffee you wanted." She indicated the half-full carafe on the warmer. "Sugar is in the bowl above, milk and cream are in the fridge."

"Can I get you some?" he asked.

"No, I'm fine, thanks."

While he doctored his coffee, she measured out flour and sugar and cocoa powder.

"What are you making now?"

"Brownies."

"One of *my* favorites," he told her.

She laughed. "Did you skip breakfast?"

"As if my grandmother would let me," he chided, stealing another cookie.

She put a wooden spoon in his hand and steered him toward a pot on the stove containing the butter and chopped semisweet chocolate she'd measured earlier. She turned the burner on to medium-low. "Just keep stirring gently until the ingredients are melted and blended."

He sipped his coffee from one hand and stirred, as instructed, with the other. "I think I have a talent for this."

"Just so long as you keep your fingers out of it."

"I'll try to resist." He caught her as she moved past him and hauled her back for a quick kiss. "But only the chocolate."

"I'm going to have to send you out of the kitchen if you continue to distract me," she warned him.

"I like kissing you."

She felt her cheeks flush. "Stir."

He resumed stirring.

She had expected that Trey would end up being more of a hindrance than a help, but aside from stealing the occasional kiss at the most unexpected times, his presence really did help move things along quickly. He willingly measured, chopped and mixed as required and without complaint.

Rita called home just after two o'clock to tell Kayla that the auction was over and that they were going for dinner in Missoula and would be home late. It was only then that Kayla realized she hadn't given any thought to dinner—or lunch. She immediately apologized to Trey for not feeding him, which made him laugh, because he'd been steadily sampling the cookies and bars while they worked.

"But you're probably starving," he realized. "You haven't touched any of this."

"I had a brownie," she confessed.

"A whole brownie?"

"It's not that I'm not tempted," she admitted. "But most of this stuff would go straight to my hips."

His gaze slid over her body, slowly, appraisingly. "I don't think you need to worry."

Kayla half wished her mother could have been there to hear what he said, except that she wouldn't have invited him to help her with the baking if her mother had been home.

"But cookies probably aren't a very healthy dinner," he continued. "Do you want to go out to grab a bite?"

She should offer to cook something there so they could sit down and talk, but the truth was, after standing around in the kitchen most of the day, her feet and back were sore, and the idea of sitting down and letting someone else prepare a meal was irresistible. "I do," she decided.

Of course, going out with Trey meant giving up another opportunity to tell him about their baby, because she didn't dare whisper the word *pregnant* within earshot of anyone else in town. She might have control over what appeared in the Ramblings column, but the Rust Creek Falls grapevine had a life of its own.

They went to the Ace in the Hole. The bar wasn't one of Kayla's favorite places, but it did have a decent menu and wasn't usually too busy on a Sunday night.

It wasn't until they were seated in the restaurant that she thought to ask, "Your grandparents weren't expecting you home for dinner?"

"I called them while you were getting changed and told them that I was going out."

She didn't ask if he'd mentioned that he was going out with her—she wasn't sure she wanted to know. Whether or not Melba had deliberately called about the pickles to force her path to cross with Trey's, as he believed, she suspected it would be dangerous to encourage the older woman's matchmaking efforts.

Especially when she was worried enough about getting her own hopes up. Yes, she had to tell Trey about the baby, but she'd thought it might be easier if they knew one another a little better. But as they were getting to know one another, she was letting herself get caught up in the ro-

mance of being with him—talking and flirting and kissing. For a girl with extremely limited dating experience,
he was a fantasy come to life. A fantasy that she knew
would come crashing down around her when she told him
that she was pregnant.

And she wasn't ready for that to happen. Not yet.

After their meal, Trey drove Kayla back to the Circle D.

He wasn't anxious to say good-night to her, but he could
tell that she was tired. She'd been on her feet in the kitchen
all day, having started her baking hours before he showed
up, and was obviously ready for bed.

Of course, thinking about Kayla in bed stirred his memories and his blood and made him wish that she didn't still
live in her parents' home—or that he wasn't staying with
his grandparents.

He'd been back in town a little more than a week—
barely nine days—but she'd been on his mind each and
every one of those days. No one he knew would believe it
if he told them that he'd spent the day in the kitchen with
Kayla, but the truth was, he didn't care what they were
doing so long as he was with her. And when he couldn't
be with her, he was thinking about her.

Now that he knew her a little better, he wondered how
he could have been so blind as to overlook her for so many
years—even if she was his best friend's little sister. Because she was also a smart and interesting woman with
hair as soft as the finest silk, eyes as blue as the Montana
sky and a smile that could light up a room. And when she
smiled at him, she made him feel like a superhero.

No other woman had ever made him feel that way. No
other woman had ever made him feel as good as he felt
when he was with her. He loved touching her and holding
her and kissing her. In recent years he'd had a few rela-

tionships, but for some reason, those had been short on the simple things—like kissing and hand-holding.

He and Kayla had already made love, and he wanted to make love with her again, but for now, he was enjoying the kissing and hand-holding and just being with her.

He was also taking a lot of cold showers.

As enjoyable as it was to spend time with Kayla, she also got him stirred up. But he was determined not to rush into anything. Not this time. He wasn't a teenager anymore—or under the influence of spiked wedding punch—and he was determined to take things slow, to show Kayla that she was worth the time and effort.

Kayla didn't tell Trey that she'd been asked to help out at the elementary school, but when she showed up at the gymnasium at three o'clock, he was there, anyway. Of course, there were a lot of people there. With the pageant scheduled for the following weekend and much work still to do, the teachers had obviously tried to pull in as many extra hands as they could.

Apparently Trey had been asked to contribute his, as he was already hammering a set together, Natalie was working on costumes—and flirting with Gavin Everton, the new gym teacher—while Kayla was put to work painting scenery.

She felt perspiration bead on her face as she stretched to paint stars in the night sky. She was wearing leggings and an oversize flannel shirt, and while the bulky attire did a good job of disguising the extra pounds she was carrying, it also ratcheted up her internal temperature considerably.

She swiped a hand over her brow. "It's warm under these lights."

"Why don't you take off that flannel shirt?" Trey suggested.

"Because I'm only wearing a camisole underneath," Kayla told him.

He grinned. "And the problem?"

She waved her paintbrush at him. "Don't you have to go hammer something?"

He lifted the tool in acknowledgment and returned his attention to the set he was building.

On the pretext of retrieving a box of lace and ribbon, Natalie sidled over to her friend. "How do you resist jumping his bones?" she asked.

"It's not easy," Kayla admitted.

"So why don't you give in and share all the details with your friends who have no romantic prospects and need a vicarious thrill?"

"Because I want what Kristen has with Ryan," she admitted. "A happily-ever-after, not just a holiday fling."

"I want a happily-ever-after someday, too. But in the meantime, I'd settle for a little happy-right-now."

"Is that why you were chatting up the new gym teacher?"

Natalie's gaze shifted to the man in question. "He's cute," she acknowledged. "But not good fling material."

"How can you tell?"

"Residential address."

"What does that mean?"

"He lives in Rust Creek Falls, which means that a casual hookup could—and very likely would—result in awkward encounters after the fact."

"Or maybe a relationship," Kayla suggested.

Natalie shrugged. "Maybe. But the risk might be greater than the reward."

But when Gavin came over to ask Natalie for her help untangling the strings of candy garland that would line the path to the Land of Sweets, she happily walked away with him.

Over the next few hours, many more people came and went, giving a few hours of their time, including Paige Traub, Maggie Crawford, Cecelia Pritchett and Mallory Dalton. Both Paige and Maggie had young children, and as Kayla picked up on little bits and pieces of their conversation, she wished she didn't feel compelled to hide her pregnancy. She wanted to be free to join in their circle and listen to their experiences and advice.

Instead, she was on the outside, alone with her questions and fears. A soon-to-be single mother still afraid to tell even the father of her baby about the baby.

She capped the paint, dropped her brush into the bucket to be washed and wiped her hands on a rag.

Trey must have finished his assigned task, too, because he closed up the toolbox and made his way over to her. "My stomach's telling me that we worked past dinner."

"Your stomach would be right," she confirmed.

"Why don't we head over to the boarding house to see what my grandmother cooked up tonight?"

Kayla brushed her hands down the thighs of her paint-splattered pants and shook her head. "I'm not going anywhere dressed like this."

"I think you look beautiful."

She looked at him skeptically. "I think someone must have hit you in the head with your hammer."

He smiled as he wiped a smear of green paint off her cheek. "Do you really have no idea what you do to me?"

"What do I do to you?" she asked warily.

"You tangle me up in knots inside."

"I'm…sorry?" she said, uncertain how to respond to his admission.

"I don't need you to be sorry," he told her. "I need you to stop taking two steps back every time we take one step forward."

She frowned. "Is that what you think I'm doing?"

He looked pointedly at the floor so she could see that she had—literally—done exactly that.

He stepped forward again.

She forced herself to hold her ground.

"Good." He framed her face in his hands and, despite the presence of several other people still lingering in the gym, lowered his mouth to hers. "That's a start."

Chapter Nine

While Kayla seemed to be resisting Trey's efforts to get closer to her, he also knew she had a hard time saying no to anyone who asked for help. The elementary school production was a case in point. So instead of asking her if she wanted to take a trip into Kalispell to go shopping with him, an invitation that he suspected she would politely decline, he stopped by the ranch the next day and said to her, "I need your help."

Not surprisingly, she responded, "With what?"

"Christmas shopping."

"I'm sure you're perfectly capable of shopping."

"You'd think so," he acknowledged. "But the truth is, I suck at shopping even worse than I do at wrapping."

She managed a smile. "I'm not sure that's possible."

"It is," he insisted. "I never seem to know what to buy, and on the rare occasion that I have a good idea, I end up with the wrong size or color."

"That's why vendors introduced gift receipts."

"We had a deal," he said, reminding her of the bargain he'd extracted from her in exchange for keeping her identity as the Rust Creek Rambler a secret. Not that he would ever have betrayed her confidence, but he wasn't opposed to using the leverage she'd given him to spend more time with her. "And I'll buy you lunch."

She sighed. "You're right—we had a deal. You don't have to bribe me with lunch."

"You'll earn it," he promised, as she followed him out to his truck. "I have a couple of things for my grandparents, but I've just found out that Hadley and Tessa are coming to Rust Creek Falls for the holidays, and I don't have a clue where to start finding something for either of them."

"What about your parents and your brothers—are they coming, too?"

He shook his head. "Not this year."

"Isn't it strange, not being with your own parents for Christmas?"

"Not really," he said. "Because when we were kids, we were always at Grandma and Grandpa's. It would seem stranger to me not to be here."

"I guess that makes sense," she agreed. "Okay, tell me about the cousins you need to shop for."

"They're Claire's older sisters. Both of them live in Bozeman. Hadley is a twenty-nine-year-old veterinarian who never turns a stray away from her door. Tessa is a twenty-seven-year-old graphic designer and movie buff."

Half an hour later, they were at the shopping center. She moved with purpose and though she claimed not to have anything specific in mind, she assured him she would know when she found what she was looking for. Since he honestly didn't have a clue, he was content to let her lead the way.

For Hadley, she found a set of glass coasters with etched

paw prints that somehow managed to be both elegant and fun. For Tessa, she found a book of iconic movie posters that he knew his cousin would love. As they exited the bookstore, he couldn't help but be impressed by her efficiency.

"I bet you're one of those people who has all of her shopping and wrapping done by the first of December, aren't you?" Trey asked her.

"Not the first," she denied. "But I don't believe in leaving things to the last minute, either."

"It's still ten days before Christmas," he pointed out.

"Apparently, we have different opinions of what the last minute is."

"Apparently," he agreed. "So tell me—have you sent your letter to Santa yet?"

She shook her head. "I think the big guy's going to be kept busy enough meeting the demands of those under the age of ten."

"Is that how old you were when you stopped believing in Santa?"

"Who says I stopped believing in Santa?"

His brows lifted.

She shrugged. "Santa made Kristen's wish come true this year."

"Huh?"

So she told him about Ryan riding in the parade as Santa Claus and his subsequent proposal to her sister.

"My grandparents told me that she was engaged, but they didn't tell me how it happened."

"Well, that's how it happened," Kayla said.

"It was pretty quick, don't you think? I mean—they only met in the summer."

She shrugged. "I guess when you know, you know."

He wondered if that was true—if that was the real reason he hadn't stopped thinking about Kayla since the night they spent together. He'd never believed there was one woman who was the right woman for him—why would he want to narrow down his options when there were so many women in the world? But since the summer, he hadn't thought about anyone but Kayla; he hadn't wanted anyone but Kayla.

"Okay, so now that Hadley and Tessa are taken care of—what about Claire?"

"I've got that one covered," he told her. "Grandma and Grandpa have booked a weekend at the Thunder Canyon Resort for Claire and Levi, and I got Claire a gift certificate for the spa."

"She'll love that," Kayla said, sounding surprised by his insight and thoughtfulness.

"That's what my grandmother said when she suggested it."

She laughed, then stopped abruptly in front of the display window of a store called Christmas Memories. She tapped a finger on the glass. "Speaking of your grandmother."

His gaze followed to where she was pointing. "Um… that's a Christmas tree."

She rolled her eyes. "What's *on* the tree?" she prompted.

"Ornaments," he realized.

She nodded, already heading into the store.

There weren't just ornaments displayed on trees but boxes of them stacked high and baskets overflowing. There were classic ornaments and fun ornaments, sports-themed and movie-themed decorations, baubles that lit up or played music—or lit up *and* played music. And there was even a selection of imported mouth-blown glass ornaments.

She held up a delicate clear glass sphere with a gold angel figurine inside. "What do you think?"

"I think I'll be the favorite grandchild this Christmas," he told her, grinning. "She'll love it so much that she'll probably rearrange all of the other ornaments on the tree so that it's hanging front and center."

"I doubt she has that much time on her hands."

"You're right—she'll make my grandfather do it."

Kayla chuckled as he took the ornament to the register to pay for it.

"Now you're all done except for the wrapping," she told him, as they exited the store.

"Oh, yeah." He made a face. "I forgot about the wrapping part."

"Do you have paper? Bows?"

"My grandmother has all of that stuff."

"You can't wrap your grandmother's gift in paper that she bought," Kayla protested.

"Why not?"

"Because you can't."

"That's not a reason."

"Yes, it is," she insisted.

"Okay, so I'll pay for the gift-wrapping service down the hall for her gift and use her paper for the rest."

Kayla shook her head. "You can bring the gifts to the ranch and I'll help you wrap them."

"Really? You'll help me?"

"I'll fold your corners—you're in charge of the tape."

He didn't manage to avoid Derek at the Circle D later that day. When they got back from shopping, Kayla sent him to the kitchen to set up at the table while she went to get her wrapping supplies. His steps faltered when he saw his friend standing at the counter, filling his thermos with coffee from the carafe.

"What are you doing here?" Derek asked, his tone more curious than concerned.

He held up the bags of gifts in his hands. "Kayla offered to help me with my wrapping."

"When did she do that?"

"When we were shopping."

"My sister went shopping with you? How did that come about?"

"I asked her."

"Why?"

"Because I needed some help figuring out what to buy for my cousins." Although that was partly true, the real truth was that he'd used the shopping as an excuse to spend time with her, and he was deliberately tiptoeing around that fact. He didn't want to tiptoe around it—he didn't want to keep his relationship a secret from anyone, especially his best friend. "And because I like her."

Derek frowned. "What do you mean—you *like* her?"

"I mean she's smart and fun and I enjoy spending time with her."

"How much time have you been spending with her?" Kayla's brother wanted to know.

"As much as possible," he admitted.

"I thought you were seeing someone in Thunder Canyon."

"I only said I was seeing someone," Trey pointed out. "You assumed that someone was in Thunder Canyon."

Derek's scowl deepened. "Are you telling me that you're *dating* my sister?"

He nodded.

"Dammit, Trey. I thought we were friends."

"We are friends."

"You can't date a friend's sister—it makes everything awkward."

"I'm sorry."

"Sorry enough to back off?" Derek challenged.

"No," he replied without any hesitation.

"How long has this been going on?"

Trey thought back to the night of the wedding but decided that didn't count—or even if it did, he had no intention of mentioning it to Kayla's brother. "A couple of weeks."

Derek shook his head as he capped his thermos. "I suppose I should be glad you didn't hook up with the blonde that night we were at the bar," he said, and walked out the door.

"What blonde in the bar?"

He winced at the sound of Kayla's voice from behind him. "Heard that, did you?"

"And I'm still waiting for an explanation," she told him.

"I mentioned that I went to the Ace in the Hole with your brother last week," he reminded her.

She nodded.

"Well, there were a couple of girls who invited us to join them," he explained. "Derek went to their table. I went home."

"Why didn't you go to their table?" she asked, sounding—to his surprise—more curious than annoyed.

"Because," he said honestly, "I didn't—I don't—want to be with anyone but you."

Kayla was so confused.

Trey was saying and doing all of the right things to make her believe that he wanted a real relationship with her. He'd even told her brother that they were dating. But he was only in town for the holidays, after which he would be going back to Thunder Canyon, and he hadn't said a word about what would happen between them after that.

Did she want a long-distance relationship? Did long-distance relationships ever work or were they just extended breakups? What were their other options?

If Trey asked, she would move to Thunder Canyon to be with him. She wasn't a schoolgirl with a crush anymore but a woman with a woman's feelings and desires. And she wanted a life with Trey and their baby—the baby he still didn't know anything about.

"That didn't take as long as I thought," Trey said, when she'd affixed a bow to the final gift.

"Doesn't it feel good—to have your shopping and wrapping done?"

"I can think of something that would feel even better," he said, leaning across the table to brush his lips to hers. "Why don't we go down to the barn, saddle up a couple of horses and go for a ride?"

She wasn't sure whether she was relieved or disappointed by his suggestion. "Actually, I have to go into town."

"For what?"

"I've got some things to do at the newspaper office."

"We don't have to go out for very long," Trey said.

"I'm sorry, but I really don't know how much time I'm going to need. I probably should have gone into the office first thing, but I promised to help you."

"I didn't mean to impose on your time," he said, just a little stiffly.

"You didn't," she assured him, reaching across the table to touch his hand. "I *wanted* to help, but now I need to go into town."

She wasn't surprised that he looked disappointed. He was probably accustomed to spending several hours a day on horseback in addition to the several more that he spent training horses at the Thunder Canyon Resort, and he likely missed the exercise and the routine.

"But there's no reason you can't go down to the barn and ask Derek—or Eli—" she added, not certain of the status of things between her youngest brother and his friend "—to give you a mount to saddle up."

"I didn't want to ride as much as I wanted to ride with you," Trey told her.

"I'm sorry," she said again, and she meant it. Not just because she couldn't accept his invitation but because she couldn't tell him the real reason why.

"Okay, we'll do it another time," he said. "For today, why don't I give you a ride into town?"

"Then I'd need a ride back again," she pointed out.

"And I was hoping you wouldn't see through my nefarious plan."

"That was your nefarious plan? Don't you have better things to do than play chauffeur for me?"

"Actually, I don't," he said. "There's nothing I want more than to be with you."

"Then I will accept your offer," she agreed.

It didn't take her very long at all to read and edit the copy for the next edition of the paper, but Kayla lingered in the office to give credence to her claim that it was a major task. She felt guilty about lying to Trey—and she'd panicked when he mentioned riding.

She hadn't been on a horse in almost two months. She'd read a lot of conflicting advice about the safety of riding during pregnancy. Many doctors said a clear and unequivocal no. In Montana, though, where most kids were put on the back of a horse before they started kindergarten, doctors were a little less strict. Kayla's own doctor had assured her that while it was usually safe for a pregnant woman to ride during her first trimester, because the baby was small and adequately protected by the mother's pelvic bone, after twelve weeks, the risks to both mother and child were increased.

Kayla had decided that she wasn't willing to take the risk. She might not have planned to have a baby at this point in her life, but as soon as she became aware of the tiny life growing inside her, she'd been determined to do everything in her power to protect that life. Of course, it was a little awkward to invent new and credible excuses to explain why she wasn't participating in an activity she'd always loved, but the busyness of the holiday season had supplied her with many reasons.

She was sure she would love riding with Trey, because she enjoyed everything they did together. At the same time, it was hard to be with him with such a huge—and growing—secret between them. Contrary to what her sister believed, she *wanted* to tell him about their baby, but she knew that revelation would change everything. She was enjoying the flirting and kissing, and she wanted to bask in the glow of his attention just a little while longer.

Surely there wasn't anything wrong with that—was there?

"Did Grandma run out of coffee?" Trey asked, sitting down across from his grandfather at Daisy's Donuts.

"She wanted me out of the house," Gene said. "Something about a fancy tea for her girls. But what are you doing here?"

"I wasn't invited to the fancy tea for the girls, either."

His grandfather barked out a laugh. "I don't imagine you were—but I was more interested in why you aren't with a certain pretty lady who has been keeping you company of late."

Trey didn't see any point in pretending he didn't know who his grandfather was talking about. "Kayla had some things to do at the newspaper."

"I forgot she worked there," Gene said. "Things getting serious between you two?"

He tried not to squirm. "I don't know."

Gene's bushy white brows lifted. "What the hell kind of response is that?"

"An honest one," Trey told him.

"She's not the type of girl you toy with. She's the type you settle down with."

He shifted uneasily. "I'm not ready to settle down, Grandpa."

"Why not?"

"I'm only twenty-eight years old."

Gene nodded. "You're twenty-eight years old, you've got a good job and a solid future. Why wouldn't you want to add a wife and a family to that picture?"

"Because I like the picture exactly as it is right now."

"Sometimes we don't really know what we want until we've lost it," his grandfather warned.

"And sometimes people rush into things that they later regret," Trey countered. "Like Claire and Levi."

"What do you think they regret?"

"Getting married so young, having a baby so soon."

"Do you really think so?"

He couldn't believe his grandfather had to ask that question. "Claire was barely twenty-two when she got married, and then she had a baby less than a year after that."

"And she's thriving as a wife and mother."

"Was she thriving when she packed up her baby and left her husband?"

"She was frustrated," Gene acknowledged. "Being married isn't always easy, but even though they hit a rough patch, they're still together, aren't they? Not just committed to one another and the vows they exchanged, but actually happy together."

Trey couldn't deny that they seemed happy and devoted to one another and their little girl. But that didn't mean he was eager to head down the same path.

"And I couldn't help but notice that you seem happy with Kayla," his grandfather continued.

"I enjoy being with her," he agreed cautiously.

"What's going to happen when the holidays are over and you go back to Thunder Canyon?"

"I haven't thought that far ahead," he admitted.

"Well, maybe you should, because if you think a girl as pretty and sweet as Kayla Dalton will still be waiting around for you when you finally come back again next summer, you might find yourself in for a nasty surprise."

The possibility made him scowl. "If she finds someone else and wants to be with someone else, then that's her choice, isn't it?"

"It is," Gene agreed. "I just wanted to be sure that you could live with those consequences."

"Besides, she doesn't give the impression of a woman chomping at the bit for marriage."

"Maybe she's not. On the other hand, her twin sister just got engaged and is starting to plan her wedding. That kind of thing tends to make other women think about their own hopes and dreams." Gene pushed his empty cup away and stood up.

"Do you want a refill?" Trey asked.

His grandfather shook his head. "I'm going to head over to the feed store and catch up with the other old folks. You young people exasperate me."

Trey got himself another cup of coffee while he waited for Kayla to text him to say that she was finished at the newspaper. Daisy's seemed to do a pretty steady business throughout the day, and several people stopped by his table to say hi and exchange a few words. But mostly he was left alone, and he found himself thinking about what his grandfather had said.

If you think a girl as pretty and sweet as Kayla Dalton will still be waiting around for you...you might be in for a nasty surprise.

Gene was probably right. There wasn't any shortage of single men in Rust Creek Falls, and just because Kayla hadn't dated many of them in the past didn't mean that couldn't change. As a result of her naturally shy demeanor, she'd been overlooked by a lot of guys, but since he'd been spending time with her, he'd noticed the speculative looks she'd been getting from other cowboys. He suspected several of them were just waiting for Trey to go back to Thunder Canyon so they could make a move—and the thought of another man making a move on Kayla didn't sit well with him.

He'd never been the jealous type, but he hadn't exactly been thrilled to see Kayla hug some guy the night they were talking outside the community center. She'd introduced the guy as Dawson Landry and told Trey he'd worked in advertising at the *Gazette* before he moved to a bigger paper in Billings. Dawson then told her that he'd recently moved back to Rust Creek Falls and the *Gazette* because he realized he wasn't cut out for life in the big city.

It was a simple and indisputable fact that after his holidays were over, Trey would go back to Thunder Canyon. He had a job and a life there, and he was happy with both. But he was happier when he was with Kayla. And when he was gone, Dawson would still be around.

The realization made him uneasy. He'd meant what he'd said to his grandfather—there were a lot of things he wanted to see and do before he tied himself down. So why did the prospect of being tied to Kayla seem more intriguing than disconcerting?

RUST CREEK RAMBLINGS: MISSING IN ACTION...
OR GETTING SOME ACTION?
Architect Jonah Dalton and artist Vanessa Brent both seemed intent on putting down roots in this town when they married last year. But the happy couple, who lives in the stunning house built by Jonah himself on the Triple D Ranch, has dropped out of sight in recent days, fueling speculation about their whereabouts. Have they slipped out of town for a pre-holiday getaway? Or are they sticking closer to home and family—and working toward expanding their own? Only time will tell...unless the Rambler tells it first!

Chapter Ten

The Candlelight Walk was an event to which all the residents of Rust Creek Falls were invited, and most enjoyed taking part in at least some aspect of it. At one end of Main Street, members of city council distributed lighted candles that were then carried in a processional to the other end where a bonfire would be lit, refreshments served and carols sung.

"I don't remember this," Trey admitted as he walked beside Kayla, the flicker of hundreds of candles illuminating the dark night with a warm glow that moved slowly down the street toward the park.

"It's a fairly new Rust Creek Falls tradition," Kayla told him.

His brows lifted. "Isn't new tradition an oxymoron?"

"I guess it is," she agreed. "Maybe it would be more accurate to say it's a recent ceremonial event that the townspeople have embraced."

"The people of this town find more excuses to get together than anyone I've ever known."

She smiled as she looked around the crowd, recognizing so many familiar faces. "That's probably true. The flood was an eye-opener for all of us, a reminder that everything we take for granted can be taken away. Even those whose homes were spared weren't immune to the effects on the community. As a result, it brought everyone closer together."

He looked around, too, and saw Shane and Gianna heading in their direction. He lifted a hand to wave them over.

"I swear, Gianna looks more pregnant every time I see her," he commented to Kayla. His friend's wife was hugely pregnant—her baby bump plainly evident even beneath the heavy coat she wore.

"When is she due?"

"I have no idea."

"Don't you and Shane work together at the resort?"

"Sure, but I'm in the stables and he's in the kitchen, and guys don't talk about stuff like that."

She rolled her eyes as his friends drew nearer.

"I didn't realize you were still in town," Trey said. "Are you staying for Christmas?"

"We are," Shane confirmed. "With both my sister and brother here now, it seemed the easiest way to get the whole family together for the holidays. Even my parents are coming—they're flying in on the twenty-second and staying at Maverick Manor."

They talked some more about holiday plans, with Gianna admitting that she was already more excited about *next* Christmas, when they would be celebrating the occasion with their baby.

"Staying with Maggie and Jesse and witnessing first-hand the havoc a child can wreak, I'm not quite so eager," Shane admitted.

"Well, it's not as if you can change your mind now," his wife pointed out. Then, to Trey and Kayla. "Madeline has made both of us realize that you can't learn parenting from a book. No matter how much you think you know, a child will quickly prove you wrong."

"Of course, the child in question is my sister's daughter," Shane interjected. "Which might explain a lot."

Kayla smiled at that.

"You guys are going to be fabulous parents," Trey said.

"Do you think so?" Gianna asked, obviously seeking reassurance.

"Of course," he agreed.

"We're both so afraid that we're going to screw something up," she admitted.

"We're going to screw a lot of things up," Shane said. "We just have to hope that our child makes it to adulthood relatively unscathed."

His wife shook her head. "And he wonders why I worry."

"Right now I'm worried about getting you back to the house and off your feet."

"As if my belly wasn't big enough, my ankles are swelling, too," Gianna explained.

Kayla and Trey exchanged good-nights with the other couple, then moved away in the opposite direction.

"Are you okay?" Trey asked. "You seemed to get quiet all of a sudden."

"I was just thinking about Gianna and Shane," she told him.

"What about them?"

"Your assurance that they're going to be fabulous parents," she admitted. "Not that I disagree—I guess I'm just wondering how you can be so sure, how anyone can know how they'll deal with parenthood before they're actually faced with the reality of it."

"Maybe no one can know for sure, but the odds are in their favor because they love one another and their unborn baby."

She nodded, envying the other couple that. She agreed that their commitment and support were important factors in parenting—and wished that she could count on Trey for the same. Of course, she couldn't expect him to support her through the pregnancy and childbirth when he still didn't know that she was pregnant. "They're certainly excited about impending parenthood, notwithstanding the challenges," she noted.

"They've been married two and a half years and are ready to enter the next stage of their life together."

"Could you ever imagine yourself as excited about becoming a father as Shane is?" she asked, striving to keep her tone light and casual.

Trey's steps faltered anyway. "What kind of a question is that?"

She shrugged. "I'm just wondering whether you've ever thought about having kids of your own."

"Well, sure," he finally said. "Someday."

"Someday?"

"There's a lot I want to do before I'm hog-tied by the responsibilities of marriage and babies."

Hog-tied?

Kayla stopped in the middle of the street and turned to look at him. "Is that how you view a family—as something that ties you down and limits your opportunities?"

"I don't mean it as if it's a bad thing," he explained. "It's just not something I'm ready for right now. Especially when I look at my parents—married thirty-two years with five kids born within the first seven years of their marriage. No, I'm definitely not in any rush to go down that same path."

She nodded, pretending to understand, but inside she felt as if her fledgling hopes—and her fragile heart—had been crushed like a candy cane beneath the heel of his boot. There was no way she could be with a man who would feel tied down by her and their baby—no way she could even tell him about their baby now.

She'd had such high hopes for their relationship a few hours earlier. While they'd walked through the town, hand in hand, she'd let herself dream that they would always be together. When she saw Nate Crawford with Noelle perched on his shoulders, she'd imagined that would be Trey with their baby in a couple of years. But now that she knew how he really felt about the prospect of fatherhood, she knew she had to end their relationship before she got in any deeper.

"It's starting to snow," she noted. "Which means it's time for me to be heading home."

"It's only a few flakes," he pointed out. "And we haven't even roasted marshmallows on the bonfire yet."

"A few flakes is all it takes for my mother to worry."

"Well, we don't want that to happen," he said, guiding her to his truck.

She felt his hand on her back, even through the thick coat she wore, and felt tears sting her eyes as she accepted she would never feel his hands on her again. Whatever fantasies she'd spun about living happily-ever-after with this man and their baby weren't ever going to be.

He helped her up onto the passenger seat and she murmured her thanks.

"Are you sure everything's okay?" he asked her.

"I'm sure," she said. "I'm just really tired." And she was—not just physically but emotionally exhausted. Not eager to make any more conversation, she fiddled with the radio until she found a station playing Christmas music, then settled back in her seat, concentrating on the song and holding back the tears that burned her eyes.

Kayla jolted when the door opened and a blast of cold air slapped her face. "What—"

"You're home," Trey told her.

She blinked. "Did I fall asleep?"

"You did," he confirmed.

"I'm sorry."

"I should apologize to you for keeping you out past your bedtime."

She managed a wan smile. "It isn't really that late," she acknowledged. "I've just had so much on my mind— so many things still to be done before Christmas—that I probably haven't been getting enough sleep."

"Then I should let you get inside to bed," he said.

She nodded. "Thanks for the ride."

He didn't take the hint. Instead, he took her arm and guided her to the front door. "Will I see you tomorrow?"

"I don't know," she hedged, aware that she needed to start putting space between them. A lot of space. Three hundred miles would be a good start, but she knew that wouldn't happen until after Christmas.

And right now, Trey seemed more focused on eliminating the space between them. "I'll call you in the morning and we'll figure it out," he said.

Then he leaned in to kiss her, but before his lips touched hers, the porch light clicked on. He pulled back just as Rita Dalton poked her head out the front door.

"What are you two doing outside in this cold weather?" she chided. "Why don't you come on in for some of the hot chocolate I just took off the stove?"

"I'm sure Trey is anxious to get back to town before the snow gets any worse," Kayla told her mom.

"It's just a few flakes," he said again.

Rita smiled at him and stepped away from the door so that they could enter.

"It's so nice that you're here to spend the holidays with Melba and Gene," Rita commented to Trey, as she busied herself pouring the steaming liquid into mugs.

"There's nowhere I'd rather be," he admitted. "And spending time with Kayla has been an added bonus on this trip."

"I know she's been enjoying your company," Rita said. "Her happy glow has brightened up the whole house these past few days."

Kayla kept her gaze focused on the mug she held between her hands and resisted the urge to bang her head against the table.

Could her mother be any more obvious in her matchmaking efforts? And how would she react if Kayla told her that *happy glow* wasn't a consequence of Trey's company but his baby in her belly? Would her mother think the man sitting at her table and drinking hot chocolate was so wonderful if she knew he'd knocked up her daughter?

"Do you have any specific plans for tomorrow?" Rita asked him, setting a plate of cookies on the table.

"Not yet," Trey said, reaching over to touch Kayla's hand. "Although I was hoping to talk Kayla into taking a drive into Kalispell with me so we could go ice skating in Woodland Park."

"Oh, that sounds like fun—doesn't it, Kayla?"

"It does," she agreed. "But I've got to put the finishing touches on the sets for the elementary school holiday pageant tomorrow."

"But you've been working on those sets all week," her mother pointed out. "Surely you can take a day off."

"Actually, I can't. The pageant is tomorrow night."

"Well, maybe we can go skating the day after," Trey suggested.

"Maybe," she agreed.

Rita frowned at her daughter's noncommittal response before she turned her attention back to their guest. "Tell me about your plans for Christmas—is your grandmother cooking a big meal with all the trimmings?"

"Of course."

"She usually serves it around midday, doesn't she?"

"Everyone is expected to be seated at the table at one o'clock sharp," he confirmed.

"We don't eat until six," Rita said. "If you wanted to join us later in the day for another meal."

Kayla felt as if she was watching a train wreck in slow motion—she could see what was happening, but she was powerless to stop it. Not an hour after she'd vowed to put distance between herself and Trey as the first step toward ending their relationship, her mother had invited him to Christmas dinner. On the other hand, spending Christmas with a girlfriend's family was probably too much of a commitment, so she felt fairly confident that he would decline the invitation.

But just in case, she decided to nudge him in that direction. "Mom, you're talking about Christmas Day," she pointed out. "I'm sure whatever plans Trey has with his family will keep him busy throughout the afternoon."

"And if they don't, I'm just letting him know that he's welcome to come here," Rita replied.

"Thank you, Mrs. Dalton. I appreciate the invitation and I'll see what I can do."

"Well, I'll leave you two to finish your beverages," she said.

"Thanks for the hot chocolate and the cookies," Trey said.

Rita beamed at him. "Anytime, Trey."

The next night Kayla attended the holiday pageant at the elementary school. The night after that she was busy helping Nina and Natalie assign and wrap gifts from the Tree of Hope for the area's needy families. It was the day after that—Saturday—while Kayla was hiding out in her room after breakfast that her sister came in.

Kristen had been so busy with the theater and wedding plans that she hadn't been at the ranch very much over the past couple of weeks.

"Trey came to see me yesterday," Kristen announced without preamble.

Kayla's head whipped around in response to her sister's casual announcement. "Why?"

"Because he's trying to plan a special surprise for you and wanted my help."

"What kind of surprise?" she asked, both curious and wary.

Kristen rolled her eyes. "If I told you, it wouldn't be a surprise, would it?"

"Then why did you mention it?"

"Because he mentioned to me that you've been so busy he hasn't seen you since the night of the Candlelight Walk, and I know for a fact that you haven't been any busier than usual and certainly not too busy to spend time with Trey if you wanted to spend time with Trey."

"Okay, so I don't want to spend time with Trey," she acknowledged.

"I don't understand," Kristen said. "Everyone can see

that the man is head over heels for you, and I know how you feel about him, so why are you avoiding him now?"

"Because I finally realized that we want different things."

"What different things?"

"A family, for starters."

Kristen frowned.

So Kayla found herself telling her sister the whole story of that night, from the candle-lighting to their encounter with Gianna and Shane and Trey's subsequent denouncement of marriage and everything that went along with it.

"Wait a minute," Kristen said. "Are you telling me that Trey still doesn't know about the baby?"

"How could I tell him?"

"How could you not?" her sister demanded. "Kayla, the man has been spending every possible minute with you over the past couple of weeks—*everyone* knows he has feelings for you. Except, apparently, the Rust Creek Rambler."

Kayla's eyes filled with tears. "Even if he does have feelings for me, how can I be with a man who doesn't want our baby?"

Her sister was silent for a long moment. "You don't know that he doesn't want your baby," she finally said. "You're making an assumption based on his response to a vague and seemingly hypothetic question. You can't hold that response against him."

"He compared being married to being hog-tied."

"He's still the father of your baby." Kristen's tone was implacable. "And even if you think you can get through the holidays without him finding out about your pregnancy, what's going to happen afterward? What are you going to tell people when they want to know the identity of your baby's father? And even if you refuse to name him, what's going to happen when Trey comes back to Rust Creek Falls and sees you with a baby? Do you really believe he won't immediately know the child is his?"

"Maybe he won't," Kayla argued, albeit weakly. "Maybe he'll want to think it's someone else's baby so that he doesn't have to be tied down by the responsibilities of parenthood."

"There's no maybe," Kristen said. "Because you're going to tell him."

Kayla sighed, but she knew her sister was right.

And maybe her dreams had been crushed, but at least now she had no expectations. Trey had made his feelings clear, and she was going to tell him about the baby without any illusions that he would want to be part of their life, and she would make it clear that she didn't want or expect anything from him. She was simply doing him the courtesy of telling him that she was pregnant.

She was admittedly a little late with that courtesy, but she would tell him.

"Tonight?" Kristen prompted.

"I can't tonight," Kayla said. "Russell called this morning. He's down with the flu and asked me to fill in for him at the theater this afternoon."

"Then tomorrow," her sister said firmly.

"Tomorrow," she agreed.

But when the curtain fell after the matinee, Kayla found Trey waiting for her backstage, and her heart gave a jolt—of surprise and longing. And when he smiled at her, her knees went weak.

Despite what she'd said to her sister about their wanting different things, she couldn't deny that she still wanted Trey. She managed to smile back, though her stomach was a tangle of nerves and knots.

"What brings you to the Kalispell Theater?"

"I decided to take your advice and check out the play," he told her.

"What did you think?"

"I was impressed. I didn't expect a small theater production to be so good."

"The actors are all spectacular," Kayla agreed. "But Belle steals the show."

Trey chuckled. "Your sister does have a flair for the dramatic."

"Speaking of my sister, I'm supposed to meet her outside her dressing room. She's waiting to give me a ride home," she explained.

"Actually, she's not—Kristen knows that I'm here to kidnap you."

"Kidnap me?"

"Well, I'm not going to throw you over my shoulder and carry you off against your will, but I asked Kristen to help me figure out a way to spend some time with you, and this was the plan we came up with."

The *surprise* that her sister hadn't given her any details—or warning—about. "Are you going to tell me anything else about this plan?"

"You don't like surprises?" he guessed.

"I guess that would depend on the surprise."

"How does a romantic dinner and a luxury suite at a local B and B sound?"

"It sounds like you've thought of everything—except what I'm going to tell my parents about where I am."

"They think you're spending the night at your sister's place," he told her, taking her hand. "I just wanted us to have some time together—just the two of us—away from all of our well-meaning but nosy family and friends in Rust Creek Falls."

"It's a good plan," she said and resigned herself to the

fact that her promise to tell him about their baby *tomorrow* had been bumped forward to *tonight*.

Trey was having a hard time reading Kayla.

She was going through the motions, but her attention seemed to be a million miles away. The restaurant he took her to for dinner had been highly recommended for both its menu and ambience. The lighting was low, the music soft and the service impeccable. His meal was delicious, and Kayla assured him that hers was, too, but she pushed more food around on her plate than she ate, and although she responded appropriately, she didn't attempt to initiate any conversation.

Needless to say, by the time he pulled into the driveway of the bed-and-breakfast, he was certain that he'd made a mistake—he just wasn't sure where. Was it the surprise aspect that she objected to? Would she have preferred to be involved in the planning? Or was she worried about his expectations? Did she think that because he'd paid for the room and dinner he'd expect her to get naked to show her appreciation?

He suspected it might be the latter when he opened the door to their suite and she caught sight of the enormous bed that dominated the room. And yeah, when he'd made the reservation he'd hoped they might share that bed, but he knew there was a sofa bed in the sitting area if Kayla decided otherwise.

He guided her past the bed to the sofa and sat her down. "What's going on, Kayla? What did I do wrong? Because it seems obvious to me that there *was* something."

"You didn't do anything wrong," she said. "Not really. It's just that… I've come to the realization that we want different things."

"What are you talking about?"

"I want what **Shane** and Gianna have," she told him. "I want to fall in love and get married and have a family."

"So? I want those things, too."

"'Someday,'" she remembered.

"And when I think of that someday, I think I'd like it to be with you."

That announcement gave her pause. "You do?"

"I do," he assured her. "I'll admit the whole conversation threw me for a loop, and it's probably going to be a while before I'm ready for marriage and babies, but please don't give up on me—on us."

Then he held out his hand to her, and Kayla gasped when she saw her teardrop earring sparkling against his palm.

"Ohmygod. I can't believe..." Her words trailed off as her eyes filled with tears. "I thought I'd lost it forever."

"I've been carrying it around with me since July," he told her. "Waiting for the right time to give it back. I should have returned it sooner. I did plan to give it back to you the next day, but you seemed so embarrassed by what happened between us."

He'd been carrying it around with him? Why? Was it possible that night had meant as much to him as it had to her? Or was she reading too much into his words because she wanted his gesture to mean more than it did?

"I was embarrassed because I thought you didn't remember," she admitted.

"I was fuzzy on the details," he acknowledged. "But I knew it was your earring and how it ended up in my bed."

She lifted the delicate piece from his palm. "Thank you. It's not worth a lot of money, but it used to be my grandmother's and it means a lot to me."

"I have to admit, when I found it in my sheets, I felt a little bit like Prince Charming after the clock struck midnight—except I had an earring instead of a shoe."

She knew that accessories weren't the only difference between her life and that of the fairy-tale princess, and yet his claim of wanting a future with her gave her hope that her story with Trey might also have a happy ending. But she knew that wasn't possible until she was honest with him about what had happened at the beginning.

"Will you give me another chance?" he asked her.

She looked around the room, noting the flowers and candles, the bottle of champagne chilling on ice. He wouldn't have gone to so much effort if he didn't think she was worth it, but would he still think so if he knew the truth she'd kept from him for so long?

"There's something I have to tell you—something that's going to change everything."

"What are you talking about?"

"I should have told you a long time ago—I wanted to tell you. But I was afraid that it would change how you felt—"

"Nothing is going to change how I feel about you," Trey said. "I promise you that."

She shook her head. "Don't. Please, don't make promises you can't keep."

"I don't know what's going on here, but you're starting to scare me," he admitted. "So whatever it is, I wish you'd just tell me so that we can deal with it."

She buried her face in her hands. "I'm messing this up."

"What's wrong, Kayla? Are you—" He hesitated, as if he didn't even want to ask the question. "Are you sick?"

"No, I'm not sick." The words were little more than a whisper as she lifted tear-drenched eyes to his. "I'm pregnant."

Chapter Eleven

Trey took a step back. Actually, it was more of a stumble than a step, which probably wasn't surprising, considering that he felt as if the rug had been pulled right out from beneath him.

"What did you say?"

"I'm pregnant."

His gaze dropped to her stomach, hidden behind yet another oversize sweater. She smoothed a hand over the fabric to show the slight but unmistakable curve of her belly.

Holy crap—she really was pregnant.

His knees buckled, and he dropped to the edge of the sofa.

"When…how—" He shook his head at the ridiculousness of the latter question. "Is it…mine?"

She nodded.

His stomach tightened painfully. "So you're—" he mentally counted back to the wedding "—five months along?"

She nodded again.

"Five months," he said again, shock slowly giving way to fury. "You've kept your pregnancy from me for *five months*?"

Kayla winced at the anger in his tone. "I didn't realize I was pregnant until the beginning of October."

"October," he echoed. "So you've only kept it a secret for the past three months?"

"I haven't told anyone because I was waiting to tell you first."

"Really? Because I think if you wanted to tell me, you would have picked up a phone and called."

Her big blue eyes filled with tears. "You don't understand," she said, her tremulous voice imploring him to try.

"You're damn right I don't understand. If the baby you're carrying really is mine—"

She gasped. "How could you doubt it's true?"

"How can I doubt it?" he demanded incredulously. "How can I believe anything you've told me when you just admitted that you've deliberately kept your pregnancy a secret for three months?"

She lifted her chin. "You have every right to be angry, but you should know me well enough to know that I wouldn't lie about my baby's paternity. And I wouldn't have spent the past couple of weeks agonizing over how to tell you if the baby wasn't yours."

"I *am* angry," he confirmed. "And obviously I don't know you as well as I thought because I never would have imagined you'd keep something like this from me."

"Please, Trey," she said. "Listen to me. Give me a chance to explain."

"I'm listening," he said, but his tone was grim, and his attention was focused on the screen of the cell phone that he'd pulled out of his pocket. His thumbs moved rapidly over the keypad, then he skimmed through the information that appeared. "We can be married right away, without any waiting period required."

Her eyes widened. "You want to get married?"

"Under the circumstances, I can't see that what I want is relevant right now," he said.

"You don't *want* to get married," she realized, her gaze dropping away. "You're only trying to do the right thing."

"Of course I'm trying to do the right thing." He looked at his phone again. "Come on—there's an office in Kalispell where we can get a license."

"It's Saturday night, Trey."

"So?"

"So I doubt very much if the county clerk's office is open right now."

He scowled. "I didn't think about that."

"And even if it was open…I'm not going to marry you."

"Why not?" he demanded.

"Because it's not what you want."

"None of this is what I want," he admitted. "But we've only got a few more months until the baby is born, and there's no way any child of mine is going to be illegitimate."

"Illegitimate is only a label," she pointed out.

"And not a label I want applied to my child."

"I'm not going to marry you, Trey."

Something in her quiet but firm tone compelled him to look at her. The stubborn set of her shoulders and defiant tilt of her chin warned him that she was ready to battle over this, although he didn't understand why. "You don't have a choice in the matter."

"Of course I do," she countered. "You can't force me to marry you."

"Maybe I can't, but I'm willing to bet your father—and your brothers—can and will."

At that, some of her defiance faded, but she held firm. "They would probably encourage a legal union, under the circumstances," she acknowledged. "But they're hardly going to demand a shotgun wedding if it's not what I want."

"You're saying you don't want to marry me?"

Her gaze slid away, her eyes filling with fresh tears. "I don't want to marry you—not like this."

The words were like physical blows that left him reeling. He didn't understand why she was being so unreasonable. She was carrying his child, but she didn't want to marry him? Why the hell not? What had he done that she would deprive him of the opportunity to be a father to his child?

And how could he change her mind? Because he had no intention of accepting her decision as final. But he also knew that he couldn't talk to her about this anymore right now. There was no way they could have a rational conversation about anything when his emotions were so raw.

He turned blindly toward the door.

"Where are you going?"

"I don't know," he admitted.

"Please, Trey. Let's sit down and talk about this."

He shook his head, his fingers curling around the doorknob. "I can't talk right now. I need some time to try to get my head around this."

And then he was gone, and Kayla was alone.

She sank down onto the sofa, her heart aching, and put a hand on the curve of her belly. "I'm sorry, baby, but I guess it's just going to be you and me."

She wasn't really surprised. She'd always expected it would be like this. From the moment she'd realized she was pregnant, she'd anticipated that she would be on her own—a single mother raising her child alone.

Over the past couple of weeks, she'd let herself imagine that things could be different. Spending time with Trey, she'd got caught up in the fantasy, believing that they were a couple and, with their baby, could be a family.

Except that wasn't what he wanted. Not really. But he had asked her to marry him—and for one brief shining moment, the dream had been within her grasp.

And she'd let it slip through her fingers.

She heard the sound of his boots pounding on the steps, fading away as he moved farther away from her.

Would he have stayed if she'd agreed to marry him?

It was what she wanted, more than anything, to marry the man she loved, the father of her child. But she'd meant what she said—she couldn't do it. Not like this. Not because he was feeling responsible and trapped. Not without knowing that he loved her, too.

And right now she was pretty sure he hated her.

But she couldn't let him storm off with so much still unresolved between them. She understood that he needed time, that he needed to think. But she suspected that if she let him go now, she could lose him forever. No—it would be better for them to talk this through. It was her fault that they hadn't done so before now, but she wasn't willing to put off their conversation any longer.

She pushed herself off the sofa and turned quickly toward the door, determined to go after him.

But she'd barely risen to her feet when the room started to spin, then the floor rushed up to meet her.

Trey was beyond angry. He was thoroughly and sincerely pissed off—possibly at himself as much as at Kayla.

He felt like a complete idiot.

Pregnant.

Since *July.*

And she hadn't said a single word to him.

Not. One. Single. Word.

Worse—he'd been completely and frustratingly oblivious. Despite all the time he'd spent with her over the past few weeks, despite the numerous times he'd kissed her and the countless times he'd held her, he hadn't had a clue.

Her assurance that no one knew about her pregnancy didn't make him feel any less like an idiot. He should have wondered about her sudden preference for baggy clothes, her unwillingness to go horseback riding with him and her determination to keep him at a physical distance. But he hadn't, and the revelation of her pregnancy had completely blindsided him.

How was he going to share the happy news with his family? If it was, indeed, happy news. *A baby.* His head was still reeling, his mind trying to grasp not just the words but what they meant to him, to his life.

He yanked the steering wheel and pulled over to the side of the road. *Christ.* He was going to be a father. Him. And he was so completely unprepared for this his hands were shaking and his heart was pounding.

Have you ever thought about having kids?

Had it only been three days ago that she'd asked him that question, after they'd seen Shane and Gianna in town after the Candlelight Walk? At the time, he'd thought the question was out of the blue—now he knew differently. She'd been trying to figure out his feelings, anticipate his reaction to the news that he was going to be a father.

And what had he said? How had he responded to her question about whether he wanted to have kids? "Someday," he'd acknowledged. A lackluster response that he'd immediately followed with, "There's a lot I want to do before I'm hog-tied by the responsibilities of marriage and babies."

He dropped his head against the steering wheel.

He'd actually compared being married to being hog-tied—no wonder she hadn't replied with an announcement of her pregnancy and confetti in the air. He couldn't have screwed things up any worse if he'd actually tried.

And what was he supposed to do now?

He had no clue.

He was surprised by the sudden urge to want to talk to his father. Maybe that was normal for a man who'd just learned he was going to be a father himself, but he couldn't begin to imagine how that conversation might proceed. No doubt his father would be completely stunned—although perhaps not so much by the news of his impending fatherhood as the identity of the mommy-to-be. Because who would believe that sweet, shy Kayla Dalton had gotten naked with serial dater Trey Strickland?

When he thought about it, even he continued to be surprised by the events of that night. And especially the repercussions. Because one of his first clues that they'd done the deed was the condom wrapper he'd discovered on the floor beside the bed the next morning. Obviously they'd taken precautions to prevent exactly this scenario, and yet, it had happened. Condom companies advertised their product as ninety-eight percent effective, but the baby Kayla was now carrying proved that they'd beaten those odds.

Unless she was taking advantage of his memory lapse from that night to make him think—

No. As frustrated and angry and hurt as he was—and despite his own question to her—he knew that Kayla wouldn't lie about something like that. There was no doubt that she was pregnant or that it was his baby. She wouldn't have agonized over how and when to tell him if she was perpetrating some elaborate ruse.

She was pregnant.

More than five months pregnant.

With his child.

Nope—it didn't get any easier thinking it the second, third or even the tenth time, and he wasn't sure he'd be able to say it aloud to anyone else, especially his father. Would his parents be disappointed in him? He was sure they would accept and love their grandchild, but he didn't think they'd be particularly proud of his actions. Not in July and not now.

They would definitely expect him to do the right thing by his child—which meant marrying the child's mother. Surprisingly, the prospect of marriage didn't scare him half as much as impending fatherhood. But he knew Kayla was scared, too, and he realized that it really didn't matter who had said or done what on the Fourth of July or even in the time that had passed since then. What mattered was what they were going to do now—and they needed to figure that out together.

Now that he'd had a little bit of time to get his heart rate down to something approximating normal, he could acknowledge how difficult it must have been for her to face him and tell him that their impulsive actions that night had resulted in a pregnancy. Especially after he'd told her that he wasn't eager to be a father.

But was it really fair for her to judge him on a response he'd given when he'd assumed she was speaking hypothetically? Because the idea of a baby, without any context, would probably scare the hell out of any guy. Not that a real child was any less terrifying than a hypothetical one, but the idea of having a child with the woman he loved—because over the past couple of weeks, he'd gradually come to accept that he did love Kayla—was almost as exciting as it was terrifying.

Maybe he'd been a little high-handed in his assertion

that they needed to get married, but he did *want* to marry her. He *wanted* to be a father to their child.

Okay—there. He didn't feel like the vise around his chest was tightening. In fact, he could almost breathe again.

His first glimpse of that subtle curve beneath her sweater had thrown him for a loop, but the ability of the female body to grow and nurture another human being was amazing. And the realization that Kayla was carrying *his* baby was both awesome and humbling.

He wondered how big the baby was now, whether she could feel it moving. Would he be able to feel it kicking inside her? Suddenly, he wanted to.

He thought about his friend, Shane, how excited he was about his baby and how he was always touching his wife's swollen belly. Trey had been happy because his friend was happy, but he didn't really get it. Now—barely an hour after he'd learned that he was going to be a father—he finally did.

Gianna was due to give birth in early February which—Trey did a quick count on his fingers—was only a few months before what he estimated was Kayla's due date. It would be kind of cool for their kids to grow up together—except that might not happen if he wasn't able to convince Kayla to marry him.

Obviously, they still had a lot of details to work out. She had a home and a job in Rust Creek Falls, and he lived and worked in Thunder Canyon. If they were going to raise this child together—and he refused to consider any other possibility—they needed to be together.

The light snow that had been falling when he left the bed-and-breakfast had changed—the flakes were coming heavier and faster now, but he wasn't concerned. He had all-wheel drive and snow tires on his truck. What he didn't have was any particular destination in mind, so when he turned onto a street filled with shops, he decided to park and walk for a while.

He tucked his chin in the collar of his jacket and walked with his head down. The wind was sharp and cold but he didn't really notice—everything inside him felt numb. At the end of the block, he found himself standing outside a jewelry store, the front window display highlighting a selection of engagement rings.

He impulsively opened the door and stepped inside.

Apparently he wasn't the only one who had decided to ignore the inclement weather. There was a man about his own age looking at bangle-style bracelets, a woman browsing a selection of watches and an older gentleman perusing engagement rings with a much younger woman.

He found what he was looking for almost immediately. The vintage-style was similar to the earrings she'd been wearing the night of the wedding, and he knew the delicate design crusted with diamonds would suit her. The clerk, visibly pleased with the quick sale, wished him a Merry Christmas and happy engagement—Trey wasn't counting on either but he was going to give both his best effort.

The weight of the ring was heavy in his pocket as he considered how and when to propose to her again. He thought she would appreciate a traditional proposal, despite the fact—or maybe because—nothing else about their relationship had been traditional. From their first kiss at Braden and Jennifer's wedding, they'd followed their own timetable. They'd fallen into bed together before they'd even gone out on a date, and now she was pregnant and showed no indication of wanting to marry him. But he was determined to change her mind on that account.

He had to brush a couple of inches of snow off his windshield before he could pull out onto the road, which was also covered with snow. The driving wasn't difficult but it was slow, and he was eager to get back to the inn, back to Kayla.

He was ready to talk to her now, eager to tell her that he was happy about their baby. He was still scared, but he was excited, too, and he wanted to share all of his thoughts and feelings with her.

But when he got back to the bed-and-breakfast, she wasn't there.

He tried calling her cell, but there was no answer. He didn't know where she could have gone—she didn't have a vehicle. And he couldn't imagine that she would have ventured outside to go for a walk in this weather. He went back downstairs, to check with Jack and Eden Caffrey, the owners of the inn. It was then that he found their note.

Kayla had a little bit of a fainting spell, so we took her to the hospital to be checked out.

Now his heart was racing for a completely different reason.

"I really am fine," Kayla told Eden, who had been hovering over her since she found her guest sprawled on the floor of her third-floor guest room.

She'd tried to resist the woman's efforts to get her to go to the hospital, because she really did feel fine, but in the end, worry about her baby won out. Jack had driven the car while Eden sat in the back with Kayla, just to be sure everything was okay. And except for a few minutes while the doctor performed his exam and then to get Kayla a snack from the cafeteria, Eden had not left her side. Jack was there, too, but he was tucked into a chair in the corner, working in a crossword puzzle book he'd brought in from the car.

She glanced from Eden's worried face to the doctor's calm facade. "Please, Dr. Gaynor, tell them that I'm fine."

"She's fine." Her ob-gyn—who had conveniently been making rounds when Kayla was brought in to the hospital—echoed the words dutifully.

"And she can go home now," Kayla prompted hopefully.

The doctor smiled as she shook her head. "I'd prefer to keep an eye on you a little bit longer, just to ensure the slight cramping you experienced earlier has truly subsided."

She sighed as she turned her attention back to Eden. "I know you must be anxious to get back. Please don't feel as if you have to stay here with me. I can catch a cab back to the inn when the doctor finally okays it."

"We run a bed-and-breakfast," Eden reminded her. "And there are a lot of hours until breakfast."

"I'll be back to check on you in a little while," Dr. Gaynor said.

Trey entered the room as she was leaving.

Jack set his book and pencil aside and rose to his feet, offering his hand to the other man. "I see you got our note."

"I did," Trey confirmed. "Thank you for taking care of Kayla."

"Of course."

Kayla eyed Trey warily as he moved closer to the bed. He'd been so angry when he left, but she didn't hear any evidence of that in his voice now.

He touched his lips to her forehead, and the sweetness of the gesture made her throat tighten.

"How are you?"

She swallowed. "I'm okay."

"I'm so sorry I wasn't there."

"It's okay," she said, but she couldn't look at him when she said it. She understood why he'd been angry and upset, but she was still hurt by his abandonment of her. Reasonable or not, his walking away had felt like a rejection of not only her news but of herself and their child, too.

He turned to Eden and Jack again. "I'm so grateful you were there, and that you brought Kayla here."

"It's lucky that she knocked the lamp off the table when she fell, or we might not have known that she fainted."

"I'm not sure I really fainted," Kayla said. "I just felt dizzy for a minute."

"And didn't remember what had happened when I found you," Eden said. "Because you fainted."

"But I'm fine now," she insisted.

"The doctor wants to keep her a little longer, for observation," Eden told Trey, contradicting Kayla's statement.

"I'll stay with her," he told the couple.

"Then we'll get out of your way," Jack said.

"Any special requests for breakfast?" Eden asked Kayla.

She shook her head. "I'm sure whatever you have planned will be perfect."

"Drive safely," Trey said to Jack. "The snow is really blowing out there."

"My honey does everything slow and steady," Eden assured him, adding a saucy wink to punctuate her statement.

Jack shook his head. "We'll see you both in the morning," he said, putting his hand on his wife's back to guide her toward the door, quietly chiding her for "embarrassing the poor fellow."

"She did embarrass you, didn't she?" Kayla asked. "Your cheeks are actually red."

"It's cold and windy outside," he told her.

"They weren't that red when you walked in a few minutes ago."

"Okay," he acknowledged. "Now let's talk about you. Are you really okay?"

"How many times do I have to say it before people start believing it?"

"Maybe a hundred more."

She eyed him warily. "How are *you*?"

"I'm okay."

She lifted her brows; he smiled.

"What about...is the baby...okay?"

"The baby's fine. Apparently, he's well-cushioned in there."

"He?"

She shrugged. "Or she."

"You don't know?"

"I didn't want to know." She played with the plastic hospital bracelet on her wrist. "Do you want to know?"

"I don't mind being surprised."

Chapter Twelve

Kayla eyed him skeptically. "Really?"

"Okay—I know that's not what I was saying earlier," Trey acknowledged. "But I'm not sure I've ever been hit with a surprise of quite that magnitude before."

"I would hope not," she admitted, managing a small smile.

He reached for her hand, linked their fingers together. "I'm sorry."

She swallowed. "Sorry that I'm pregnant?"

"No." He squeezed her fingers. "I'm not sorry about the baby—I'm sorry that I was such an ass when you told me about the baby."

"And I'm sorry I waited so long to tell you."

"Why did you?"

"I was scared."

"Of me?"

She shook her head. "Of how you'd react."

"How did you think I'd react? Did you expect me to get mad and walk out?"

"That was one possible scenario—after you rejected the possibility that it was your baby."

He winced. "It was knee-jerk."

"I get that. But you should know that there wasn't any other possibility. What happened between us that night—I don't do things like that."

"I know."

Now it was her turn to wince. "I'm not sure if I should feel reassured or insulted."

He chuckled. "Rust Creek Falls is a small town," he reminded her. "You have a reputation for flying under the radar."

"Obviously, no one saw me do the walk of shame out of the boarding house the morning after Braden and Jennifer's wedding."

"Walk of shame? Because you spent the night with me?"

"Because I don't do things like that," she said again.

"I kind of hoped we'd do it again sometime."

"Like maybe this weekend?"

"Like maybe this weekend," he acknowledged. "But that isn't why I brought you here. I really did just want to spend some time with you away from all of the demands and distractions of our families."

"It was a sweet gesture."

He winced. "Sweet?"

She chuckled softly then sighed. "I really wanted to tell you," she insisted. "But every time I tried to lead into the conversation, something else came up."

"Nothing that was more important than what you weren't telling me," he pointed out.

She nodded, silently acknowledging his point. "The

first time was the day we had lunch—when Claire called and asked you to pick up diapers."

He did remember that his cousin's call had interrupted something Kayla started to say, and he winced when he remembered some of the things he'd said when he'd explained the errand request to Kayla. "Okay, I guess that one's on me."

"And then there was the night we were wrapping Presents for Patriots and you told me we had time to figure out everything we needed to know about one another."

"Only because I didn't know then that our time would be limited by the arrival of a bundle of joy."

"And then when we ran into Shane and Gianna after the Candlelight Walk."

"When I said that I wasn't looking to be a father anytime soon," he realized.

She nodded.

"You really should have just blurted out the news before I had a chance to make such an ass of myself."

"I'll keep that in mind if I ever find myself in this predicament again."

"You won't," he told her. "Our next baby—"

Whatever else he was going to say was interrupted by a knock at the door.

Kayla let out a breath—a sigh that was part relief and part frustration—when a technician pushed a trolley cart into the room.

"I'm Judy," she said. "Dr. Gaynor asked me to stop by so we could take a look at your baby."

Kayla's hand tightened on his. "Is something wrong?"

"There's no reason to think so," the technician assured her. "The doctor just wants to double-check before she releases you."

"Okay." But she didn't relinquish her viselike grip of Trey's hand.

Judy lifted the hem of Kayla's shirt and pushed down the top of her pants to expose the curve of her belly. She squirted the warm gel onto her tummy then spread it over her skin with the wand attached to the portable ultrasound machine.

A soft whooshing sounded, and the screen came to life, but Kayla found herself watching Trey, whose attention was riveted by the image that appeared.

"Is that…our baby?"

"That's our baby," she confirmed.

"It's…wow."

She understood exactly what he was feeling: the complete array of emotions that filled his heart. Awe. Joy. Fear.

She understood because it was the way she'd felt the first time she'd seen tangible evidence of the life growing inside her, not just the outline of the baby's head and torso or the little limbs flailing around, but the tiny heart inside her baby's chest that seemed to beat in tandem with her own.

"Everything looks great," Judy said. "Your baby is measuring right on target for twenty-four weeks."

"What does that mean?" Trey asked. "How big is he? Or she?" he hastened to add.

"Approximately eleven and a half inches long, probably weighing in at just under a pound—about the size of an ear of corn."

"Less than a pound?" Kayla wasn't happy. "I've gained more than ten, and you're telling me that less than one of that is my baby?"

The technician chuckled. "But all of it is necessary—there's also the placenta, amniotic fluid and various other factors that contribute to mother's weight gain during pregnancy."

"So it's not the hot chocolate with extra whipped cream?"

"It's not the hot chocolate," Judy promised. "Even with extra whipped cream." She continued to move the transducer over Kayla's belly. "You said 'he—or she'…did you want to know your baby's sex?"

Kayla looked at Trey. "Do you?"

"Do *you*?"

"I am a little curious," she admitted. "Especially because my sister seems convinced—on the basis of no scientific evidence whatsoever—that it's a boy."

Trey frowned at that but didn't comment, and Kayla realized he was probably unhappy to discover that her sister had known about the pregnancy before he did. But she wasn't going to explain or apologize—not in front of the ultrasound tech—and she was grateful that all he said to Judy was, "We'd like to know."

"The aunt-to-be is right," Judy told her. "It's a boy."

When Dr. Gaynor finally returned and approved Kayla's release, Trey insisted on bringing his truck right up to the exit doors of the hospital so that she didn't have to walk across the snowy ground to the parking lot. She appreciated his solicitousness, but she also knew his apparent acceptance of her pregnancy didn't mean anything was settled between them.

The earlier blizzard-like conditions had passed and the plows had already been out to clear the main roads, so the drive back to the bed-and-breakfast was quick and uneventful.

Throughout the short journey, her mind was so preoccupied with other things that she'd almost forgotten they weren't heading back to Rust Creek Falls. She knew that Trey would take her home if she asked, but she also knew that running away was a cowardly thing to do. They had to figure out their plans for the baby together so they could tell both of their families.

But back in their room at the inn, her gaze kept being drawn to the big bed at its center—the bed she'd hoped to share with Trey. The bed she still wanted to share with Trey, because apparently her active pregnancy hormones didn't care that there were unresolved issues so much as they remembered how much fun it had been to make a baby with this man and wanted to do the deed again.

She moved past the bed to the sitting area and lowered herself onto the edge of the sofa.

"Do you need anything?" Trey asked. "Are you hungry? You didn't eat very much at dinner."

She shook her head. "Eden got me some fries and gravy from the hospital cafeteria before you arrived."

"French fries and gravy?"

"Pregnant women have some strange cravings," she said, a little defensively.

"Anything else you've been wanting? Pickles? Ice cream? Pickles and ice cream?"

"No—at least, not at the same time," she assured him. "But if you're hungry, maybe Eden will let you sneak into the kitchen to make a sandwich."

She'd no sooner finished speaking when there was a knock on the door. Trey went to answer it and returned with a silver tray in his hands.

"Apparently Eden thought we might both be hungry," he said, setting down the tray set with a plate of cheeses and crackers, another of crudités and dip and a bowl of fresh fruit.

"They're both lovely people," Kayla said. "And this house is spectacular. How did you find it?"

He nodded. "Gage Christensen recommended it."

"You haven't stayed here before?"

"No." He selected a grape from the bowl, popped it into his mouth. "Did you think this was my usual rendezvous spot in Kalispell?"

She lifted a shoulder.

"I know I had a reputation in high school—and maybe for some years afterward—but I'm not that same guy anymore. And I didn't bring you here because there was a bed and none of our family within spitting distance. I brought you here because I wanted to give us a chance to reconnect without all the other craziness of our lives interfering."

"And the bed?" she prompted.

"I might have had hopes," he admitted. "But no expectations."

He plucked another grape from the bowl, offered it to her. She took the fruit from his fingertips, bit into it. The skin was crisp, the juice sweet. "Oh!"

"What is it?" Trey dropped the strawberry he'd selected. "What's wrong?"

"Nothing's wrong." She took his hand and laid it on the curve of her belly.

His brows drew together. "What...oh."

She knew then that he'd felt it, too, the subtle nudges against his palm that were evidence of their baby moving around inside her.

His lips curved and he shifted his hand to one side to make room for the other, splaying both of his palms against her belly. "Now I know why Shane's always touching Gianna's stomach."

The baby indulged him with a few moments of activity before settling again.

"It's fascinating," he said. "To know there's a tiny human being inside there. A baby. *Our* baby."

She smiled at the wonderment in his tone. "Our baby boy," she reminded him.

His hands moved from her belly to link with hers. "Do you know why I came back?"

"Hopefully because you didn't plan on returning to Rust Creek Falls with me stranded here."

"I didn't," he assured her. "But I meant why I came back when I did."

She shook her head. "Why did you come back when you did?"

"Because I realized that I love you."

For a moment, her heart actually stopped beating. Then it started racing. "You…what?"

"It kind of snuck up and surprised me, too," he admitted. "Maybe because I didn't ever expect to feel this way again. But it's true, Kayla. I love you."

She looked at their intertwined fingers and willed her heart to stop acting crazy for a minute so that she could think.

"This would be a great place to say that you love me, too," he prompted.

And she did love him. Maybe she always had. But she wasn't yet ready to put her heart on the line simply because he'd said the three little words she'd often dreamed he might one day say to her. Especially when she couldn't help but question the timing and his motives.

"I'm not sure that you're feeling what you think you're feeling," she said gently.

He scowled. "You don't believe I'm in love with you?"

"I think you *want* to believe you're in love with me because that would make the situation more acceptable to you."

"Kayla, there is nothing about this situation that is the least bit *un*acceptable to me."

"Six hours ago, the idea of being a husband and father totally freaked you out, and I understand that—"

"I'm not freaked out," he told her.

She lifted her brows.

"Okay, I *was* freaked out," he admitted. "Because the possibility that the one night we spent together might have created a baby never crossed my mind, and finding out not only that you were pregnant but more than five months pregnant was a little bit of a shock.

"But once I had some time to think about it—once my brain got past the holy-crap-I'm-going-to-be-a-father part and began to focus on the I'm-having-a-baby-with-Kayla part—I realized that I was okay with this."

"You're okay with it?" she echoed dubiously.

"I'm not explaining myself very well, am I?"

"I don't know," she admitted. "But if you're trying to reassure me, I'm not feeling very reassured."

"I wouldn't have planned for you to get pregnant that night," he said. "As I'm sure it wasn't in your plans, either."

"Definitely not," she agreed.

"But then I realized that if this had to happen—if a condom had to fail—I'm glad it was with you."

"That sounded…almost poetic," she decided, touched by the sincerity in his tone even more than his words.

"I want to be a father to our baby. I really do."

"I want that, too."

He was tempted to show her the ring right then and there, to prove how serious he was about wanting to be with her, but he suspected it was too soon to ask her again to marry him. If she needed some time to be sure of him and his feelings, he would give her that time.

Because the next time he proposed, he wasn't going to accept any answer but yes.

It wasn't really late, but it had been a long and emotionally draining day, and when Trey caught Kayla attempting to stifle a yawn, he said, "Why don't you go get changed and crawl into bed?"

"I don't have anything to change into," she realized.

"Your sister packed you a bag. I brought it up to the bedroom when I checked in before I went to the theater."

"I'm not sure I want to know what she packed for me," Kayla admitted, but she went into the other room to find out.

She was right to be suspicious. The silky short nightshirt and matching wrap certainly weren't from Kayla's closet, but since they were all she had, she put them on, then brushed her hair and cleaned her teeth.

When she was finished, she heard the television from the sitting area and saw that Trey was stretched out with his feet on the table and his eyes half-closed. She hesitated inside the doorway, and his eyes slowly opened and slid over her with a heated intensity that felt like a physical caress.

"I like what your sister packed," he murmured.

"This isn't mine," she blurted out.

"It looks good on you."

She tightened the belt around her waist, not realizing how the movement emphasized the curve of her belly until she saw his gaze drop and linger there.

"I think I understand your sudden affinity for shapeless clothing."

"I've gained ten and a half pounds already," she admitted.

"You're growing our baby."

"You didn't stumble over the words that time."

"I'm going to stumble," he told her. "This is all new territory for me."

"Me, too."

"But you've had a little bit more time to get used to the idea than me."

She didn't know if he'd intended the words as an accusation, but she couldn't help but interpret them as such, and she nodded in acknowledgment. "And more time to panic."

He'd been so shocked about the news of her pregnancy—and then so angry at her for keeping it from him—that he hadn't really considered how she'd felt, the gamut of emotions she must have experienced when she first suspected and then confirmed that she was going to have a baby. "Were you scared?"

"Terrified," she admitted without hesitation.

And she'd been alone.

But that had been her choice. She could have contacted him—could have shared her worries and her fears. Instead, she'd chosen to keep her pregnancy from everyone, including her baby's father.

"I didn't want to believe it was even possible," she said to him now. "I'd always thought I was so smart, that there really wasn't any such thing as an unplanned pregnancy anymore."

An understandable assumption considering that they'd taken precautions—and the reason for his own initial disbelief.

"I was so sure that my period was only late, but I went to a drugstore in Kalispell and bought a pregnancy test that I took into a public restroom. And I cried," she admitted softly. "I was so scared and confused. I couldn't do anything but cry."

He hated knowing that she'd been afraid and alone. Maybe she could have called him—*should* have called him—but he'd been three hundred miles away.

And maybe he should have shown some initiative and called her. Even if he'd had no reason to suspect there were any repercussions from the night they'd spent together, he should have kept in touch with her. By not doing so, he'd relegated their lovemaking to the status of a one-night stand.

"I'm sorry."

"I think we both need to stop saying that."

"I don't think I can say it enough," he said. "I totally screwed up. I should have—"

Determined to silence his self-recrimination, Kayla leaned forward and touched her lips to his.

Her kiss had the intended effect of halting his words, and the added benefit of clouding her own brain. Especially when he drew her closer and deepened the kiss, sliding his tongue between her lips to parry with her own.

Her hormones kicked into overdrive. She didn't know if it was a side effect of the pregnancy or just being with Trey, but she couldn't deny that she wanted him.

She slid her hands beneath his shirt, over the smooth skin and taut muscles. She felt his abs quiver beneath her touch. She wanted to feel his skin against hers, his body inside hers. She reached for the button of his jeans and was surprised—and disappointed—when he caught her wrist.

"I'm not sure that's a good idea," he told her.

"I disagree." She pressed her lips to his throat, just below his jaw, where his pulse was racing.

His hands gripped her hips. "You were just released from the hospital two hours ago."

"And when the doctor released me, she assured both of us that there were absolutely no restrictions on any physical activities."

"I'm sure she wasn't referring to…"

"To?" she prompted, amused by his inability to say the word *sex* aloud to her.

"Intimacy," he decided.

"I'm pretty sure she was," she countered. "Did you know that some women experience an increased sexual desire during pregnancy?"

"No, I…um…can't say that I did."

"And there are some women who become so hypersensitive they can't stand to be touched."

"I didn't…um…know that…either," he said, looking everywhere but at her.

"Of course, men have different responses to pregnancy, too. Some find their partners even more attractive and appealing…while others are completely turned off by the changes to her body," she said, attempting to withdraw from his embrace when he pointedly kept his gaze averted.

He let her pull back but not away. "And you think I'm turned off," he realized.

She shrugged. "You're not touching me."

"Only because I don't want to hurt you…or our baby."

"You won't," she assured him.

He drew her close again, so she couldn't possibly miss the evidence of his desire for her.

"I want you, Kayla. More than you could probably imagine."

"I don't know about that—I have a pretty good imagination," she told him. "And I want you, too."

"We were only naked together once before," he noted. "And as I recall, we were both fumbling around in the dark."

"I think we managed okay."

"This time, I want the lights on. I want to see you. And I want to take my time exploring every single inch of your sexy pregnant body," he told her.

"That sounds…promising."

"It is a promise."

Chapter Thirteen

He guided her through the doorway into the bedroom, over to the bed. He unfastened the knot at the front of her robe, parted the sides and then slid his hands over her belly and up. "Your breasts are fuller."

"I should have figured you'd notice that."

He grinned, unapologetic, as he brushed his thumbs over her nipples, through the silky fabric. She moaned softly.

"And more sensitive," he realized.

"Yes, but in a good way. You don't have to worry about touching me—I *want* you to touch me."

"I want to touch you." He pushed the robe off her shoulders, stroked his fingertips down her arms. "I am touching you."

Then he lifted the hem of her nightshirt and lowered his head so that he was kissing her. First one breast, then the other, softly, almost reverently. After he kissed the hollow between them, his mouth moved lower, to the swell of her belly.

He pulled back the covers on the bed and eased her down onto the mattress, stripping her nightshirt away in the process. She was completely naked now, and suddenly very self-conscious.

She wasn't sure how he would respond to her belly unveiled. It was one thing to look at the curve beneath the fabric of the clothes she was wearing and quite another to see the skin stretched taut and all kinds of tiny blue veins visible beneath the surface. But he didn't seem put off at all.

He stripped away his own clothes and set a small square packet on the table beside the bed.

"That's a little like closing the barn door after the horse has escaped, don't you think?" she asked.

His brow furrowed. "I guess it is," he acknowledged. "I wasn't thinking. It's just a habit."

She nodded. "I'm relieved to know it is."

"But since we're not worried about you getting pregnant, there's nothing else you need to worry about, either. I have a clean bill of health and I haven't been with anyone else since we were together."

"You haven't been with anyone else in six months?"

"I didn't want to be with anyone else—because I couldn't stop thinking about you," he told her, trailing his fingertips along the insides of her thighs, upward from her knees, silently urging her legs to part.

"I couldn't stop thinking about you, either," she admitted.

"I'm happy to hear it."

The first time they'd made love, there hadn't been much foreplay. There hadn't been any need. They'd both wanted the same thing, and she had no regrets about what happened between them that night. But she had to admit their lovemaking had been a little…she wouldn't say disappointing so much as quick.

Trey made up for it now. He took his time learning his way around her body, exploring with his hands and his lips, touching and teasing until she was so aroused she could hardly stand it. Her heart was pounding, her blood was pulsing and her body was aching, desperately straining toward the ultimate pinnacle of pleasure.

She was already close, so close, but she wanted him there with her. She wanted to feel his hard length driving into her. She shifted restlessly, lifting her hips off the bed, wordlessly seeking the fulfillment she knew he could give her. When he eased back and pushed her knees farther apart, she thought, *Yes—finally, yes.*

But apparently he wasn't as eager as she was for their bodies to join together. Instead, he lowered his head and pressed his lips to the inside of one thigh, then the other. A whimper—a tangle of frustration and need—caught in her throat as his thumbs brushed the curls at the apex of her legs.

"Is this okay?" he asked.

"Only if you're trying to make me crazy."

"I'm trying to satisfy that raging sexual desire you were telling me about."

"I didn't say it was raging," she denied, just a little primly.

He chuckled softly, then his lips were on her, nibbling and teasing, his tongue gently probing her feminine core.

"Okay…now it's raging," she admitted breathlessly.

And then it was spinning out of control.

Finally, he lowered himself over her, into her.

She closed her eyes, sighing with satisfaction as he filled her. Then he began to move, slow, deep strokes that touched her very center. Her desire was definitely raging now. He'd already given her so much pleasure, but he held back, resisting his own release until he felt her body convulse around him.

Afterward, he brushed her hair away from her face and touched his lips to her temple. "I love you, Kayla. I understand that you might need some time to believe it's true, but I hope you won't need too much time, because I'm anxious for us to build a life together."

I love you, too.

The words—his and her own—filled her heart to overflowing, but the words stuck in her throat.

She *did* love him, but until she was certain that his feelings were real and the declaration wasn't prompted by some overblown sense of chivalrous responsibility, she wasn't going to let herself trust that they were true.

Trey wasn't surprised when Kayla suggested that he could drop her off at her sister's place rather than take her home, and considering that he'd manufactured her sleepover at Kristen's house to explain her absence from the Circle D, it wasn't an unreasonable request. However, now that he knew about their baby, he didn't want to keep the news of her pregnancy from either of their families a moment longer.

Her parents were at the table, having just finished their midday meal, when they arrived. Rita immediately offered to fix a couple more plates, but Trey assured her they'd already eaten. He didn't tell her that they'd had a late breakfast at the lovely little inn in Kalispell where he'd spent the night with her daughter.

"You just missed Derek and Eli," Rita told Trey. "They were here for lunch but headed out to check the fence on the northern boundary of the property."

"That's too bad," he said, though truthfully, he was grateful. He was prepared to face Kayla's parents and share the news of her pregnancy, but he wasn't eager to witness her brother's response. Derek had been unhappy enough to learn that Trey was dating his sister; he wasn't sure what his friend would do if he knew she was pregnant.

"I'm sure they'll both catch up with you soon," Kayla said, her words sounding like an ominous warning.

"In the meantime," Trey said, refusing to be sidetracked from his purpose, "we wanted to share some news with both of you."

Rita glanced from him to her daughter and back again, her expression one of polite confusion. "What news is that?"

He glanced at Kayla, indicating that it was her turn to talk, hoping that her parents would accept the news more easily if it came from her lips.

She drew in a deep breath and tried to smile, but her lips wobbled rather than curved. "We're going to have a baby."

There was silence for a long moment before Rita finally spoke.

"You mean you're planning to have a baby sometime in the future?" she asked, clearly trying to understand a statement that made no sense to her because she had no idea of the history between Kayla and Trey.

"No, I mean I'm pregnant."

Charles set his coffee mug down on the table, hard, his grip on the handle so tight his knuckles were white. "You're the father?" he demanded of Trey.

"Yes, sir."

"I don't understand," Rita said. "How is this possible? Trey's only been in town a couple of weeks…and the two of you just started dating."

"It happened in the summer," Kayla admitted. "The baby's due in April."

Her mother's eyes shimmered with moisture. "I knew something was up with you, but I never imagined...oh, Kayla."

Her eyes filled, too. He knew she felt guilty for keeping her pregnancy a secret, and she probably felt as if she'd disappointed her parents. Beneath the table, he reached for her hand and squeezed it reassuringly.

"When's the wedding?" Charles wanted to know.

"We're still trying to figure that out," Trey said.

"What's to figure? You call a minister and set a date, and if you haven't already done so, it just means you're dragging your heels and I—"

"Daddy," Kayla interrupted. "I'm the one dragging my heels."

Charles frowned at his daughter. "You don't want to marry the father of your baby?"

"I don't want to get married for the wrong reasons."

"A baby is never a wrong reason," he insisted. "And if you did the deed with a man you don't love, that's no one's fault but your own."

A single tear slid down Kayla's cheek; she swiped it away.

"Don't you think that's a little harsh?" Rita asked.

"Reality's harsh," her husband replied.

"What's done is done," Kayla's mother said, attempting to be a voice of reason. Then, to her daughter, "Have you been seeing a doctor?"

"Yes, I've been seeing a doctor," Kayla assured her.

"And everything's okay?"

She nodded. "Everything's fine."

"Everything except that she's unmarried and pregnant," Charles grumbled.

* * *

"That wasn't so bad, was it?" Trey asked her.

"It wasn't exactly a walk in the park."

"True, but I half expected to be leaving with my backside full of buckshot so, in comparison, it wasn't so bad."

"I'm sorry that my father is pressuring you to marry me."

"You seem to have forgotten that I asked you first—that I *want* to marry you."

"You want to do the right thing," she reminded him.

"Yes, I do," he confirmed. "Lucky for me that the right thing also gives me what I want—a life with you and our child."

Now that Kayla had told her parents, it was time for Trey to tell his. But since he wouldn't be seeing them until after the New Year, he decided to face his grandparents first.

He found his grandmother in the kitchen, preparing the evening meal.

"Where is everyone?"

"Claire and Levi took Bekka for a walk, and your grandfather is in the garage trying to find replacement bulbs for the Christmas lights that he insists are packed away somewhere."

"How long has he been digging around in there?"

"Let's just say it would have been quicker for him to drive into Kalispell to buy new replacement bulbs." She looked up from the potatoes she was peeling. "Something on your mind?"

His grandmother's instincts were uncanny as usual and since he couldn't imagine an appropriate segue, he just blurted it out. "Kayla's pregnant."

"I don't believe it," she said sternly. "And you shouldn't

be spreading gossip about matters that aren't any of your business."

"It is my business," Trey told her. "It's my baby."

His grandmother put a hand to her heart. "You're joking."

He shook his head. "She's due in April. April ninth."

Melba silently counted on her fingers.

"It happened when I was here in the summer," he admitted.

"What happened in the summer?" his grandfather asked, stomping into the kitchen.

His grandmother looked at him, because it was his news to tell.

"I slept with Kayla Dalton," he admitted.

Gene winced. "Why do I need to know this?"

"Because she's pregnant."

"Didn't your father give you the talk?"

"Yes, he gave me the talk," Trey confirmed. "And you gave me the talk. And we were careful."

"Obviously not careful enough." Gene nodded to thank his wife for the coffee she set in front of him. "You're going to marry her."

It wasn't a question but a statement; Trey nodded, anyway. "As soon as I can get Kayla to agree."

"What do you mean? Why wouldn't she agree?"

Melba rolled her eyes at her husband. "Because he probably said 'we better get married' without any attempt at romance."

"Don't you think the time for romance is past?" Gene asked.

"The time for romance is never past," his wife insisted.

"I can do romance," Trey interjected, attempting to shift the attention back to the subject at hand and away from the argument he could sense was brewing between his grandparents.

"Of course you can," Melba agreed.

"Start by buying a ring," Gene advised. "That's the most important thing."

"Telling her you love her is the most important thing," his grandmother countered. "But only if it's true."

"It is. And I did."

"Then you should buy a ring."

"I did that, too."

"And she still said no?"

"I didn't have the ring when I asked," he admitted. "And I didn't know how I felt about her when I asked."

"And now she'll think you only said those words because of the baby."

"That's the root of the problem," Gene spoke up again. "Thinking."

"I beg your pardon?" his wife said.

"Young women these days overthink everything—and young men don't know when to take action."

"What do you suggest I do?" Trey wanted to know. "Throw her over my shoulder and cart her off to the preacher?"

"I don't know that your actions need to be that drastic," his grandfather allowed. "But I've got an idea."

Later that night, Kayla tracked her mother down in the laundry room. "I know you're disappointed in me, and I'm sorry," she said softly.

"I'm mostly disappointed that you didn't tell us about the baby sooner," Rita said, measuring soap into the dispenser and setting the machine to wash. "It might have been a lot of years ago, but I still remember how anxious and worried I was during my first pregnancy—actually frantic and paranoid might be more accurate. I needed reassurance about everything I was thinking and feeling and doing, and I relied so much on my mother for that advice and support."

"I wanted to tell you." Kayla picked up a T-shirt, still warm from the dryer, and began to fold it. "But I didn't think it was fair to tell anyone about the baby until I told the baby's father."

"I can understand that," her mother allowed. "I can't understand why it took you five months to do that."

"Because Trey had gone back to Thunder Canyon and it wasn't the kind of news I felt comfortable sharing over the phone." Especially after a drunken one-night stand— but, of course, she didn't share *that* part with her mother.

"So when did you finally tell him?"

She set the folded shirt aside and picked up another. "Yesterday."

Rita matched up a pair of socks. "Yesterday?"

She nodded.

"The man's been in town for more than two weeks," her mother pointed out.

She nodded again.

"Well, I can't say I know how awkward and difficult it must have been to share the news," Rita admitted. "And that's between the two of you."

Kayla continued to fold her father's T-shirts.

"You know, I wouldn't have made a big deal about the French fries if I'd known you were pregnant."

She managed a laugh. "I know, Mom."

Rita matched another pair of socks. "Trey Strickland... I never would have guessed."

"I really am sorry," Kayla said.

"I don't want you to be sorry—I want you to be happy."

"I've screwed everything up so badly, I'm not sure that's possible. Trey is so angry…and hurt."

"He wouldn't be so angry and hurt if he didn't care about you deeply," Rita told her.

Kayla considered that for a minute, wanting to believe it could be true and, at the same time, afraid to let herself hope.

"Do you care about him?" her mother prompted.

There was no point in denying her feelings any longer. "I love him."

Rita smiled. "I thought you did."

"I'm not sure that's a good thing," she admitted. "I can't separate what I want from what's best for both of us and our baby."

"It *is* a good thing," her mother insisted. "Because with love, all things are possible."

RUST CREEK RAMBLINGS: BITS & BITES
Lovely Manhattan transplant, Lissa Christensen, has been spending time with fellow newcomer and nurse, Callie Crawford—at the local medical clinic. Are the two friends catching up on local gossip…or is it possible that the sexy sheriff's wife is "in the family way"?

Kayla was relieved when she woke up on Christmas morning because it was the one day she could be fairly certain that her family would be too busy with other things to pressure her about the situation with Trey.

She appreciated that they were thinking about what was best for her and the baby, but what they didn't seem to understand was that she *wanted* to marry Trey—she just needed to know that it was what he wanted, too, and she couldn't shake the feeling that he had only proposed out of duty and obligation. Until she could be sure that he really wanted them to be a family, she couldn't say yes.

The door flew open and Kristen leaped onto Kayla's bed. "Merry Christmas, Sleepyhead."

She smiled at her twin, who had opted to sleep in her old room the night before so the sisters could celebrate Christmas morning together one last time. "Merry Christmas, Earlybird."

Kristen fell back on the mattress, so their heads were side by side on the pillow. "It's the end of an era, isn't it?"

Kayla nodded. "Next year, you'll wake up with your husband on Christmas morning."

"And you'll be celebrating your baby's first Christmas."

She nodded again. Although it was a full year away, she couldn't help wondering what the day would look like—when she and Trey would have an eight-month-old baby with whom to celebrate the holiday. But where would they be? And would they be together? Or would their baby be shuffled from one house to another from one year to the next?

"I understand why you turned down Trey's proposal," Kristen said to her now. "You didn't want to marry him for the sake of your baby. But maybe you shouldn't have looked at it that way."

"How should I have looked at it?"

"You could have focused on the fact that the man you love was asking you to marry him."

"But I don't just want to marry the man I love—I want to marry a man who loves me, too."

"And he does," Kristen said.

But Kayla wasn't so sure. Since the day after she'd told him about the baby—and after they'd told their respective families about the baby—he hadn't said another word about marriage or even hinted about wanting a life with her and their baby.

"What does he have to do to prove to you that his feelings are real?" Kristen asked her now.

"I don't know," she admitted. "But I think I deserve something more than an impulsive and slightly panicked proposal."

"You definitely do," her sister agreed.

"Girls!" Rita called up to her daughters. "Breakfast is ready."

Kayla threw back the covers. "I'm starving."

Her sister laughed. "You're always starving these days."

She walked down the stairs beside Kristen, as she'd done every Christmas morning for as long as she could remember. But this year, Kayla wasn't thinking about presents from the jolly man in the red suit—she was preoccupied with thoughts of a different man…and hoping for a holiday miracle.

Chapter Fourteen

Breakfast was fruit and yogurt, pancakes, and bacon and eggs, and for once her mother didn't give Kayla a disapproving glance when she filled her plate.

She looked around the table as she ate—at her mother and her father, still solid after thirty-five years of marriage; her brother, Jonah, and his wife, Vanessa, still newlyweds; Kristen and her fiancé, blissfully in love and eager to start their life together. She wanted what they each had—the affection and commitment—and she wanted it with Trey.

After everyone had eaten their fill and the kitchen was cleaned up, the family moved into the living room to exchange gifts. Kayla hadn't yet sat down when there was a knock at the door. Her heart quickened.

Though Trey hadn't said anything more about her mother's invitation to join them on Christmas Day, she couldn't imagine who else it might be. Certainly there wasn't anyone else that she wanted to see today as much as she wanted to see him.

"I'll get it," she said, feigning a casualness she didn't feel as she tried not to race to the door.

It *was* Trey—and he looked so incredibly handsome in a black sweater and dark jeans with his leather jacket unzipped. He hadn't shaved, but she didn't mind the light growth of ginger stubble on his jaw. In fact, she thought it made him look even sexier than usual, and just a little bit dangerous.

Dangerous to your heart, she reminded herself, stepping away from the door so he could enter.

"Merry Christmas, Kayla." He took advantage of the fact that they were out of sight of everyone else to steal a quick kiss, touching his lips lightly to hers.

"Merry Christmas," she replied, feeling suddenly and inexplicably shy. After two days of no contact except through text messages, she wasn't sure what to say or how to act around him.

"Is it okay that I'm here?"

"My mother did invite you," she reminded him.

"I meant, is it okay with you?"

"Oh. Of course."

He tipped her chin up. "I've missed you."

"You have?"

"Yes, I have," he confirmed.

"I missed you, too," she admitted.

He smiled at that. "Did Santa bring you everything you wanted for Christmas?"

Everything she wanted was standing right in front of her, but she didn't know how Trey would respond to that kind of declaration. Instead she said, "I don't know yet—we're opening gifts in the front room now."

"Then I'm just in time," he said, holding up the bag of gifts he carried.

Kayla led him into the family room where a fire crackled in the hearth and the lights were lit on an enormous tree beneath which was a small mountain of presents. After greetings and holiday wishes were exchanged all around, Derek began to distribute gifts.

The mountain had been cut down to a moderate hill when her brother passed a heavy square box to her.

Kayla frowned at the tag. "It doesn't say who it's from."

Her family looked from one to the other, all of them shaking their heads. Trey did the same when the attention shifted in his direction.

"It doesn't matter who it's from," Kristen said. "It has your name on it."

So she undid the bow and tore open the paper, but the plain cardboard gave no hint as to its contents. She lifted the lid and found a bottle of something that looked suspiciously like moonshine, beneath which was a note in spidery handwriting.

"What does it say?" Rita asked.

She started to read aloud:

"Dear Ms. Rust Creek Ramblings,

"It didn't take people long to figure out that the wedding punch was doctored but no one knows who did it…or why. Now that you and Trey are together again, I'll fill you in on the story.

    "What I saw on the Fourtth of July was more than just a happy couple ready to embark on a life together. I saw a lot of lonely people who needed a little push toward their own happiness. Or maybe more than a little push. Jordyn Leigh Cates, Levi Wyatt, Lani Dalton, Brad Crawford, your sister…and you. All of you sampled Homer Gilmore's Wedding Moonshine—and look at everyone now!

    "My work is done. Sincerely, HG"

Kayla was stunned—and already thinking that this confession would make the perfect topic of her next column.

"Homer Gilmore?" Kristen said skeptically. "He doesn't strike me as the romantic type."

"Forget Homer Gilmore," Rita said. "The old coot's clearly off his rocker to think, for even a minute, that Kayla is the Rust Creek Rambler."

"Actually, that's something I need to talk to you all about," Kayla said, her gaze hesitantly shifting around the room from one family member to the next, briefly—and apologetically—encompassing them all.

Everyone was silent for a moment, stunned by the news that sweet, shy Kayla was the source of Rust Creek Falls's juiciest gossip.

Derek recovered his voice first. "Are you saying it's true?" he demanded.

"It's true," she admitted.

"You've been writing gossip for the paper about our friends?" her father asked, his voice heavy with disapproval.

"Not just our friends but our family," Kristen noted. "You wrote about *me*! And Jonah and Vanessa, too!"

"None of it was malicious or untrue," Kayla said defensively.

"Which just goes to prove that people aren't always what they seem," Derek said, looking pointedly from his sister to his high school pal.

"There's something written on the back," Trey noted, trying to deflect attention away from Kayla's revelation and back to Homer's confession.

She turned the page over.

"PS—It was Boyd Sullivan's idea to 'lose' the farm to Brad Crawford. His broken heart just couldn't mend here in Rust Creek Falls. Since he left, he's been living in upstate New York and may have found love again. I'll never regret buying him that train ticket."

"I still can't believe Homer Gilmore could mastermind such a plan," Rita said.

"I still can't believe our daughter is the Rust Creek Rambler," Charles grumbled.

"There's something else in the box," Kayla noted, lifting out a handful of ring boxes and a stack of extra marriage licenses with another note attached. *I didn't get to use them all—maybe one will come in handy for you someday.*

"I guess that answers the question of how Will and Jordyn Leigh were able to get married so easily," Eli noted.

"I guess I should be grateful that I didn't drink any of that punch," Derek muttered.

"If you had, and if you'd actually met someone, you might be a little less cranky," Kristen pointed out.

"There are still presents to be opened," Rita noted, eager to defuse the argument she could sense brewing between her children.

Derek resumed handing out gifts.

"I have one for Kayla," Trey said, then slipped back into the foyer. When he returned, he was carrying an enormous fluffy white teddy bear with a Santa hat on its head.

"It's adorable," Kayla said, hugging the bear to her chest. Then she hugged Trey. "Thank you."

"I think he was expecting a yes or no rather than thank you," Kristen said.

In response to Kayla's blank look, she pointed to the stocking that the bear held between its paws.

On the stocking was embroidered the words "Will you marry me?"

Kayla's breath caught in her throat. She looked from the bear to Trey, who dropped to one knee beside her.

"I promised to give you some time, so that you could be sure—and know that I was sure. And I am. I love you, and what I most want for Christmas is to be your husband and a father to our baby." He reached into the stocking that the bear was holding and pulled out a small box, then flipped open the lid to reveal a gorgeous vintage engagement ring. "So I'm asking now, Kayla Dalton, will you marry me?"

She was glad she was already sitting down, because her knees had turned to jelly. When they were in Kalispell together, it had been easy to disregard his impulsive proposal because she knew he was trying to do the right thing. The fact that he'd chosen to ask her again, putting his heart on the line not just in front of her but her whole family, too, made her realize that his motivation might be a little more complicated than she'd assumed.

What did she need to believe his feelings for her were real? Only this—exactly this.

"Yes, Trey Strickland, I will marry you."

He fumbled a little as he pulled the ring from the box. "I'm not nervous about marrying you," he said, his voice lowered so that only she could hear. "I'm just feeling a little nervous about doing this in front of your whole family."

"So why did you?"

"Because I wanted to prove to you that it wasn't an impulse or an obligation. And because I thought putting a ring on your finger would increase my chances of getting out of here without my backside full of buckshot."

"I can see why you'd be concerned," she told him. "It's a really nice backside."

His brows lifted. "You think so?" He finally slid the ring on her finger and then leaned forward to kiss her softly.

Kayla almost forgot they were in a room filled with her family until everyone applauded. Trey must have, too, because he eased back and smiled sheepishly.

"Now we need to set a date for the wedding," Rita said. "And I think the sooner, the better."

"I agree," Trey said. "In fact, I was thinking today would be perfect."

"Today?" Kayla echoed. "We can't get married today."

"Why not?"

"Because there's paperwork that needs to be filed and—"

"The paperwork's done," he told her. "My grandfather suggested I take care of the administrative details so that we could have a Christmas wedding."

"You're serious," she realized. "You want to get married today."

"I don't want to wait another minute to make you my wife."

"I love the idea," she admitted. "But we need more than a license to make it happen."

"The minister is just waiting for our call."

"But… I don't even have a dress."

"I do," Kristen interjected.

"You just happen to have a wedding dress hanging in your closet?" Kayla asked skeptically, because she knew the gown her sister had ordered for her own wedding wouldn't be ready for several weeks and wouldn't fit Kayla even if she did have it.

"The theater was getting rid of some costumes, including a vintage wedding dress, so I brought it home, certain it could be put to good use one day," Kristen explained.

Kayla laid a hand on her swollen tummy. "I can't imagine anything designed for the stage would fit me in this condition."

"It has an empire waist and a full skirt," Kristen said. Still, she hesitated.

"You should at least try it," her mother suggested.

"What do you think?" she asked Trey.

"I think you're going to be the most beautiful bride ever, no matter what you're wearing."

She glanced down at the simple green tunic-style top that she had on over black leggings. "Well, I'd rather not be wearing this," she admitted.

Kristen took her hand and tugged her to her feet. "Let's go upstairs so you can try it on," she urged.

"While you're doing that, I'm going to call my grand-parents to invite them to the wedding."

"Then I guess you'd better call the minister, too," Kayla said.

"I will," he promised.

Trey made the necessary phone calls, then went in search of his high school friend and soon-to-be brother-in-law. He found Derek brooding in the corner, a long-necked bottle in his hand and a dark expression on his face.

"You're pissed," Trey realized.

"Did you expect me to be thrilled to learn that my buddy knocked up my little sister?" Derek challenged.

Trey winced. "It really wasn't like that."

"You weren't drunk on Homer Gilmore's moonshine when you seduced her?"

"The wedding punch might have been a factor," he acknowledged. "But I don't regret what happened, because I love your sister and I'm looking forward to building a life and a family with her."

"You always did have a way with words—and with the ladies," Derek sneered.

"We both did," Trey reminded his friend. "And if you

remember that, you should also remember that when I make a commitment, I honor it. I could tell you that, from this day forward, there will be no one for me but Kayla. The truth is, there hasn't been anyone for me but Kayla since that night we spent together in July."

"The fact you spent that night with her still makes me want to take you out to the barn to go a few rounds," Kayla's brother warned. "The only reason I'm restraining myself is that I know my sister wouldn't forgive me if I was the reason her groom was sporting a black eye on their wedding day."

"I appreciate your restraint," Trey said. "And I'd appreciate it even more if you stood beside me as my best man when I marry her."

Derek considered the offer for a long moment before he finally nodded. "I could do that."

Trey offered his hand. "I'm going to do everything I can to make Kayla happy—to be a good husband to her and a good father to our baby."

"I know you will," his friend agreed grudgingly. "Because if you don't, you'll answer to me."

"I can't believe the theater was going to throw this away," Kayla said, trailing a hand down the lace sleeve of the dress her sister presented to her.

"Lots of costumes and limited storage space," Kristen said matter-of-factly.

"But this is…beautiful."

"It is," her sister agreed. "And it will look even more beautiful on you."

"I'm feeling a little guilty."

"Why?"

"Because you got engaged first but I'm getting married first."

"Actually, I'm happy it turned out this way," Kristen said. "Because after you're married and your baby is born, there will be no distractions from my big day."

Kayla chuckled. "Absolutely not," she promised.

With her sister's help, she stripped down and slipped into the vintage gown.

"Maybe it wasn't just a lack of storage space," Kristen allowed, as she worked on fastening the dozens of tiny buttons that ran down the back of the dress. "It could be that this dress isn't exactly conducive to quick costume changes."

But at last she finished, then turned Kayla around to face her. "Oh, it's perfect." Kristen's eyes misted. "You're perfect. Absolutely perfect."

"You think it's okay that I'm wearing white?"

"I think a bride should wear whatever she wants on her wedding day, but it's actually off-white, so you don't need to worry about anyone wagging a finger in your direction."

"No, it's more likely tongues will be wagging."

"The joys of living in a small town," her sister reminded her. "But at least you've mostly flown under the radar of the Rust Creek Rambler for the past few years."

"Not entirely, though," she pointed out.

"Yeah, there were occasional—and completely forgettable mentions—just enough to ensure that no one ever suspected you were the author of the column."

"I protected you, too," she pointed out.

"Which is probably why people *did* suspect me."

"I guess I didn't think that one through very well," she apologized, as she pinned her hair into a twist at the back of her head.

"It didn't bother me," Kristen assured her. Then, "You need earrings."

"You're right." Kayla lifted the lid of her jewelry box

and selected the sparkly teardrops that had belonged to their grandmother.

"I thought you lost one of those."

"I did," she admitted. "In Trey's bed."

Her sister's brows lifted. "It's a good thing he found it before his grandmother did."

"No kidding," she agreed.

"When did you get it back?"

"Just a few days ago. He said he'd been carrying it with him since that morning, waiting for the right time to return it to me."

Kristen laid a hand on her heart and sighed dramatically. "Just like Prince Charming with the glass slipper."

Kayla felt her cheeks flush. "I don't know if it was just like that, but it was pretty romantic."

There was a tap of knuckles on the door, then Rita peeked her head into her daughter's room. "Everyone is here so anytime— Oh, Kayla." Her mother's eyes filled with tears. "You look so beautiful." She drew in a breath and blinked away the moisture. "But you don't have any flowers."

"I didn't expect to even have a dress," she reminded her mother. "I'm not too worried about the flowers."

"But it's your wedding day. It should be perfect."

"I'm marrying the man I love—it already is perfect."

"You're right," Rita agreed. "And speaking of men, your father would like to give you away."

"I know—he tried to do that the day he found out about my pregnancy."

Her mother flushed.

Kayla touched a hand to her arm. "I'm kidding, Mom. I would very much like to have Dad walk me down the aisle."

"Actually, it's going to be the hall, not an aisle," Kristen pointed out.

"I'll go get him," Rita said, and slipped out of the room, closing the door softly behind her.

"Are you nervous?" Kristen asked.

Kayla shook her head. "Excited. Although I'm still not convinced this isn't all a dream."

"It is a dream," Kristen said. "It's *your* dream come true. Don't question it—just enjoy it."

"I've been in love with Trey since I was twelve years old."

"I know."

"I never thought he'd even notice me, never mind love me back."

"Well, he did and he does," her sister told her. "And right now, he's waiting downstairs to marry you."

Trey shifted from one foot to the other as he waited for Kayla to appear. His grandmother had positioned him in front of the Christmas tree—insisting it would be the best backdrop for pictures—and Derek stood beside him. The minister was there, too, smiling and chatting with guests, assuring them that it wasn't an imposition but a pleasure to be called out to perform a surprise wedding ceremony, even on Christmas Day.

Trey had been in agreement with the plan—the idea of a small family wedding suited him perfectly. But apparently it wasn't going to be as small as he'd anticipated. Not only had his grandparents picked up the minister on their way to the Circle D, they'd also brought Claire, Levi, Bekka, Hadley and Tessa. And while Kayla was doing whatever she was doing upstairs to get ready for the wedding, the mother of the bride had been busy on the phone, because before the bride descended the stairs again, the living room was practically bursting at the seams with people.

There were Kayla's siblings, of course. Jonah and his wife, Vanessa, Kristen's fiancé, Ryan Roarke, and Eli and Derek. Her aunt and uncle, Mary and Ben Dalton were also there, along with their unmarried children—Anderson, Travis and Lindsay. Also in attendance were Caleb and Mallory Dalton with their adopted daughter, Lily; Paige and Sutter Traub with their son, Carter; and Lani Dalton and Russ Campbell.

Then Kayla appeared and everyone else faded away.

He'd meant what he'd said when he'd told her she would look beautiful in whatever she was wearing, but in the white dress with her hair pinned up and a pair of familiar earrings dangling from her lobes, she was absolutely stunning.

He couldn't take his eyes off her while they exchanged their vows, and he didn't want to. A few short weeks earlier, he could not have imagined that he would be married before the end of the year—certainly and not be happy about it. But as Kayla returned his promise to love, honor and cherish "till death do us part," he realized that he was finally where he belonged. It didn't matter if they were in Rust Creek Falls or Thunder Canyon or even Timbuktu—what mattered was that they were together.

Finally, the minister invited the groom to kiss his bride.

Trey lowered his head to hers, pausing before his lips touched hers to whisper, "I love you, Mrs. Strickland."

"And I love you, Mr. Strickland," she whispered back.

He smiled and then—finally—he kissed his wife for the first time.

After that, flutes of champagne and sparkling grape juice were passed around so that guests could toast the newlyweds. Kayla surprised everyone by offering a toast of her own.

"I just want to thank our families and friends who have gathered here today—on very short notice—to celebrate this occasion with us. Christmas has always been my favorite time of the year but now for even more reasons. Because of Trey, I got everything I wanted this year—and more.

"But if I could have one more wish come true, it would be that all of our siblings and cousins and friends will someday be as lucky to share the same love and happiness that I've found with Trey."

Of course, there were many more toasts after that, and everyone wanted to kiss the bride and congratulate the groom. Trey didn't really mind, but he was anxious to be alone with Kayla, and it seemed like forever before they managed to extricate themselves from the crowd to head back to his room at the boarding house.

"Why do I feel like I'm returning to the scene of the crime?" Kayla asked, after Trey had parked his truck and came around to the passenger side to help her out.

"Maybe because you're whispering and tiptoeing," he suggested.

"I feel guilty," she acknowledged.

"Why would you feel guilty?"

"Because we violated your grandparents' rule prohibiting overnight visitors."

"That was five months ago," he reminded her. "Now we're lawfully married and there's no reason to feel guilty."

"I guess it's going to take me a little while to get used to that fact."

"You've got the rest of your life—the rest of our lives," he amended, unlocking the door to his room.

"I'm looking forward to every single day of it."

"Me, too," he said. "And I promise you, now that my ring is on your finger, if you ever try to sneak out in the middle of the night again, I will go after you."

"I guess I didn't handle that very well, did I?"

"You might have saved us some confusion and a lot of lost time if you hadn't disappeared before the sun came up."

"I'm not going anywhere this time," she assured him.

"You won't have a chance—I'm not going to let you out of my arms tonight."

She smiled. "Is that a promise?"

"That is very definitely a promise."

His gaze skimmed over her, slowly, appreciatively, from the top of her head to the toes of the shoes that peeked out beneath the hem of her gown. "Your sister made a good call on this dress," he said. "You look fabulous in it, but I suspect you're going to look even better out of it."

"I'm five-and-a-half months pregnant," she reminded him.

"I know."

"I've gained twelve pounds now."

He framed her face in his hands. "You were beautiful in July, you're beautiful now, and you'll be just as beautiful in April when you can't see your swollen ankles, and even more so when we're celebrating our fiftieth anniversary," he said sincerely.

"What did I ever do to deserve you?"

"You got drunk on Homer's punch." He turned her around and began to unfasten the buttons of her dress.

She laughed softly. "I wasn't drunk. I was in love. I've been in love with you since the day you climbed the big maple tree behind my parents' house to retrieve my favorite doll that Derek had thrown into the top branches."

"I can't say I loved you then," he admitted. "But I love you now. For now and forever."

Her heart sighed with contentment—and then Trey swore under his breath.

She glanced over her shoulder.

"I changed my mind about this dress," he grumbled. "How many damn buttons are on this thing?"

"I don't know," she admitted. "Kristen did it up for me."

He struggled for a few more minutes, then finally had the back opened up enough that he could push the dress off her shoulders and over her hips. He quickly stripped away her undergarments and dispensed with his own attire in record time.

Then he slowed everything down. His lips were patient, his hands gentle, as he aroused her tenderly and very thoroughly. When she was ready for him—almost begging for him—he finally, and again slowly, eased into her. The pressure built inside her the same way—slowly, but steadily, inexorably guiding her toward the culmination of pleasure.

She was close...so close. But she needed something more than what he was giving her, more than soft touches and gentle strokes.

"Trey, please. I need—"

He brushed his lips against hers. "I know."

But he didn't, because he continued at the same leisurely pace, and while it felt good—*really* good—it wasn't enough. She bit back a whimper of frustration as the pleasure continued to build inside her, gentle rolling waves of sensation that teased her with the promise of more.

And then, just when she thought that promise was beyond her reach, her body imploded, shattering into a million little pieces that scattered like stars into the far reaches of the galaxy before they drifted back to earth. Slowly.

It was a long time later before they were both able to breathe normally again, before Trey summoned the energy to tuck her close against him.

"Wow," she said softly.

With her head nestled against his shoulder, she couldn't see his face, but she heard the smile in his voice when he said, "I never thought I'd say this—but I think I'm going to have to thank Homer Gilmore for spiking the wedding punch."

"Maybe we should name our baby after him," Kayla suggested.

"I think we should stick to saying thanks," Trey countered.

She laughed softly. "Okay—we'll do that."

"Did you have any thoughts about names?"

"No, I've tried not to think too far ahead."

"It isn't so far now," he pointed out. "Less than four months."

She shifted so that she was on her side, facing him. "I'm sorry that I didn't tell you sooner, that you missed out on so much."

"I won't miss out next time."

Though she was touched by the confident assurance in his voice, she wanted to enjoy the present with him before scheduling their future. "Could we have this baby before you start planning for the next one?"

"Of course," he agreed. "But I do think we should practice our baby-making technique."

"Again?"

He shrugged. "We missed a lot of months together—and they do say practice makes perfect."

She lifted her arms to his shoulders and drew him down to her. "In that case, we should definitely practice."

Epilogue

When Trey returned to their room at the boarding house, he found his wife exactly where he'd left her: sitting at the desk, staring at the screen of her laptop computer.

"Are you *still* working on that?"

"Just finishing up."

He set down the tray of fruit and cheese he'd snagged from the kitchen along with the two crystal flute glasses he'd borrowed from his grandparents' cabinet, then reached into the mini-fridge for the bottle of nonalcoholic champagne he'd purchased for the occasion. "That's what you said half an hour ago."

"But now it's true," she told him, turning the computer so that he could see the screen.

His brows lifted. "You're giving me a sneak peek?"

"I want an unbiased second opinion before I send it to my editor."

"Then you shouldn't ask me," he pointed out. "How

can I be unbiased about anything written by the woman I love?"

She smiled, as she always did when he told her he loved her. "True, but I want you to read it, anyway."

He stood behind her chair, his hands on her shoulders, as he read her last column for the Rust Creek newspaper.

RUST CREEK RAMBLINGS: OUT WITH THE OLD, IN WITH THE NEW (YEAR) & MISCELLANEOUS OTHER THINGS

2015 was an eventful year for the residents of Rust Creek Falls. In addition to the usual weddings and funerals, engagements and reunions, there was the mystery of the wedding punch served at the Fourth of July nuptials of Braden Traub and Jennifer Mac-Callum. A mystery that was finally solved when Homer Gilmore confessed to spiking the punch with his homemade moonshine in an effort to help the lonely residents of our fair town find their bliss. On many accounts, he succeeded.

As the hours count down and the dawn of a New Year draws ever closer, one cannot help but wonder what events will make headlines in the months ahead. I'll look forward to reading about them rather than writing them myself, as I'm leaving Rust Creek Falls to make my home in Thunder Canyon with my new husband and the family we're going to have together. But don't worry, loyal readers, there is a new Rambler already in your midst, already keeping an ear to the ground and a notepad in hand.

Happy New Year to All!
Your (former) Rust Creek Rambler,
Kayla Dalton Strickland

"You put your name on it," Trey noted with surprise.

His wife nodded. "I thought it was time for the people of Rust Creek Falls to learn the identity of the Rambler."

"You mean that you wanted them to know your sister wasn't responsible for the column," he guessed.

"That, too," she agreed.

"Are you going to miss it?"

She shook her head. "I had a lot of fun with it, but I'm more than ready to move on, to focus on being a wife and—very soon—a mother."

"No regrets about leaving Rust Creek Falls?"

"None," she assured him. "Besides, Thunder Canyon isn't really that far away, and we'll come back to visit whenever we can."

"I'm sure we'll be pressured to come back even more often," Trey said. "Especially after the baby is born."

"And no doubt there will be a convoy from Rust Creek Falls to Thunder Canyon as soon as our families hear that the baby is on his way."

"You're probably right."

She clicked SEND to submit her final edition of "Ramblings" to the newspaper, then shut down the computer.

As Trey handed her a glass of nonalcoholic champagne, she could hear the rest of the family and boarding house guests talking and laughing in the main parlor.

"Are you sure you don't want to go downstairs to ring in the New Year with your cousins and your grandparents?"

"I'm sure," he said. "I want to celebrate our first New Year together with my bride."

"But what if I want to wear a sparkly crown and blow one of those noisy horns?"

He picked up a sparkly crown—pilfered from the box of party stuff his grandmother had amassed for the celebration—and settled it on her head. Then he handed her a noisemaker.

"Once again, you've thought of everything, haven't you?"

"I tried." He touched his lips to hers. "I love you, Kayla."

Her eyes filled with tears.

He pulled back. "What did I do? Why are you crying?"

She managed to laugh at his panicked tone. "Sorry— I'm pregnant and hormonal, and I'm crying because I'm happier than I ever thought possible."

Trey wrapped his arms around her. "That's lucky for us then, because I feel the same way—well, except for the pregnant, hormonal and crying parts."

Kayla laughed again, and as the guests downstairs began their countdown to midnight, she and Trey celebrated the birth of the New Year in their own way.

* * * * *

SHE SIGHED. HE WAS very handsome. She loved the way his eyes crinkled when he smiled. She loved the strong, chiseled lines of his wide mouth, the high cheekbones, the thick black wavy hair around his leonine face. His chest was a work of art in itself. She had to force herself not to look at it too much. It was broad and muscular, under a thick mat of curling black hair that ran down to the waistband of his silk pajamas. Apparently, he didn't like jackets, because he never wore one with the bottoms. His arms were muscular, without being overly so. He would have delighted an artist.

"What are you thinking so hard about?" he wondered aloud.

"That an artist would love painting you," she blurted out, and then flushed then cleared her throat. "Sorry. I wasn't thinking."

He lifted both eyebrows. "Miss Ashton," he scoffed, "you aren't by any chance flirting with me, are you?"

"Mr. Coleman, the thought never crossed my mind!"

"Don't obsess over me," he said firmly, but his eyes were still twinkling. "I'm a married man."

She sighed. "Yes, thank goodness."

His eyebrows lifted in a silent question.

"Well, if you weren't married, I'd probably disgrace myself. Imagine, trying to ravish a sick man in bed because I'm obsessing over the way he looks without a shirt!"

He burst out laughing. "Go away, you bad girl."

Her own eyes twinkled. "I'll banish myself to the kitchen and make lovely things for you to eat."

"I'll look forward to that."

She smiled and left him.

He looked after her with conflicting emotions. He had a wife. Sadly, one who was a disappointment in almost every way; a cold woman who took and took without a thought of giving anything back. He'd married her thinking she was the image of his mother. Elise had seemed very different while they were dating. But the minute the ring was on her finger, she was off on her travels, spending more and more of his money, linking up with old friends whom she paid to travel with her. She was never home. In fact, she made a point of avoiding her husband as much as possible.

This really was the last straw, though, ignoring him when he was ill. It had cut him to the quick to have Todd and Niki see the emptiness of their relationship. He wasn't that sick. It was the principle of the thing. Well, he had some thinking to do when he left the Ashtons, didn't he?

CHRISTMAS DAY WAS BOISTEROUS. Niki and Edna and three other women took turns putting food on the table for an unending succession of people who worked for the Ashtons. Most were cowboys, but several were executives from Todd's oil corporation.

Niki liked them all, but she was especially fond of their children. She dreamed of having a child of her own one day. She spent hours in department stores, ogling the baby things.

She got down on the carpet with the children around the Christmas tree, oohing and aahing over the presents as they opened them. One little girl who was six years old got a Barbie doll with a holiday theme. The child cried when she opened the gaily wrapped package.

"Lisa, what's wrong, baby?" Niki cooed, drawing her into her lap.

"Daddy never buys me dolls, and I love dolls so much, Niki," she whispered. "Thank you!" She kissed Niki and held on tight.

"You should tell him that you like dolls, sweetheart," Niki said, hugging her close.

"I did. He bought me a big yellow truck."

"A what?"

"A truck, Niki," the child said with a very grown-up sigh. "He wanted a little boy. He said so."

Niki looked as indignant as she felt. But she forced herself to smile at the child. "I think little girls are very sweet," she said softly, brushing back the pretty dark hair.

"So do I," Blair said, kneeling down beside them. He smiled at the child, too. "I wish I had a little girl."

"You do? Honest?" Lisa asked, wide-eyed.

"Honest."

She got up from Niki's lap and hugged the big man. "You're nice."

He hugged her back. It surprised him, how much he wanted a child. He drew back, the smile still on his face. "So are you, precious."

"I'm going to show Mama my doll," she said. "Thanks, Niki!"

"You're very welcome."

The little girl ran into the dining room, where the adults were finishing dessert.

"Poor thing," Niki said under her breath. "Even if he thinks it, he shouldn't have told her."

"She's a nice child," he said, getting to his feet. He looked down at Niki. "You're a nice child, yourself."

She made a face at him. "Thanks. I think."

His dark eyes held an expression she'd never seen before. They fell to her waistline and jerked back up. He turned away. "Any more coffee going? I'm sure mine's cold."

"Edna will have made a new pot by now," she said. His attitude disconcerted her. Why had he looked at her that way? Her eyes followed him as he strode back into the dining room, towering over most of the other men. The little girl smiled up at him, and he ruffled her hair.

He wanted children. She could see it. But apparently his wife didn't. What a waste, she thought. What a wife he had. She felt sorry for him. He'd said when he was engaged that he was crazy about Elise. Why didn't she care enough to come when he was ill?

"It's not my business," she told herself firmly.

It wasn't. But she felt very sorry for him just the same. If he'd married *her*, they'd have a houseful of children. She'd take care of him and love him and nurse him when he was sick…she pulled herself up short. He was a married man. She shouldn't be thinking such things.

SHE'D BOUGHT PRESENTS online for her father and Edna and Blair. She was careful to get Blair something impersonal. She didn't want his wife to think she was chasing him or anything. She picked out a tie tac, a *fleur de lis* made of solid gold. She couldn't understand why she'd chosen such a thing. He had Greek ancestry, as far as she knew, not French. It had been an impulse.

Her father had gone to answer the phone, a call from a business associate who wanted to wish him happy holidays, leaving Blair and Niki alone in the living room by the tree. She felt like an idiot for making the purchase.

Now Blair was opening the gift, and she ground her teeth together when he took the lid off the box and stared at it with wide, stunned eyes.

"I'm sorry," she began self-consciously. "The sales slip is in there," she added. "You can exchange it if..."

He looked at her. His expression stopped her tirade midsentence. "My mother was French," he said quietly. "How did you know?"

She faltered. She couldn't manage words. "I didn't. It was an impulse."

His big fingers smoothed over the tie tac. "In fact, I had one just like it that she bought me when I graduated from college." He swallowed. Hard. "Thanks."

"You're very welcome."

His dark eyes pinned hers. "Open yours now."

She fumbled with the small box he'd had hidden in his suitcase until this morning. She tore off the ribbons and opened it. Inside was the most beautiful brooch she'd ever seen. It was a golden orchid on an ivory background. The orchid was purple with a yellow center, made of delicate amethyst and topaz and gold.

She looked at him with wide, soft eyes. "It's so beautiful..."

He smiled with real affection. "It reminded me of you, when I saw it in the jewelry store," he lied, because he'd had it commissioned by a noted jewelry craftsman, just for her. "Little hothouse orchid," he teased.

She flushed. She took the delicate brooch out of its box

and pinned it to the bodice of her black velvet dress. "I've never had anything so lovely," she faltered. "Thank you."

He stood up and drew her close to him. "Thank you, Niki." He bent and started to brush her mouth with his, but forced himself to deflect the kiss to her soft cheek. "Merry Christmas."

She felt the embrace to the nails of her toes. He smelled of expensive cologne and soap, and the feel of that powerful body so close to hers made her vibrate inside. She was flustered by the contact, and uneasy because he was married.

She laughed, moving away. "I'll wear it to church every Sunday," she promised without really looking at him.

He cleared his throat. The contact had affected him, too. "I'll wear mine to board meetings, for a lucky charm," he teased gently. "To ward off hostile takeovers."

"I promise it will do the job," she replied, and grinned.

Her father came back to the living room, and the sudden, tense silence was broken. Conversation turned to politics and the weather, and Niki joined in with forced cheerfulness.

But she couldn't stop touching the orchid brooch she'd pinned to her dress.

TIME PASSED. BLAIR'S visits to the ranch had slowed until they were almost nonexistent. Her father said Blair was trying to make his marriage work. Niki thought, privately, that it would take a miracle to turn fun-loving Elise into a housewife. But she forced herself not to dwell on it. Blair was married. Period. She did try to go out more with her friends, but never on a blind date again. The experience with Harvey had affected her more than she'd realized.

Graduation day came all too soon. Niki had enjoyed college. The daily commute was a grind, especially in the harsh winter, but thanks to Tex, who could drive in snow and ice, it was never a problem. Her grade point average was good enough for a magna cum laude award. And she'd already purchased her class ring months before.

"Is Blair coming with Elise, do you think?" Niki asked her father as they parted inside the auditorium just before the graduation ceremony.

He looked uncomfortable. "I don't think so," he said. "They've had some sort of blowup," he added. "Blair's butler, Jameson, called me last night. He said Blair locked himself in his study and won't come out."

"Oh, dear," Niki said, worried. "Can't he find a key and get in?"

"I'll suggest that," he promised. He forced a smile. "Go graduate. You've worked hard for this."

She smiled. "Yes, I have. Now all I have to do is decide if I want to go on to graduate school or get a job."

"A job?" he scoffed. "As if you'll ever need to work."

"You're rich," she pointed out. "I'm not."

"You're rich, too," he argued. He bent and kissed her cheek, a little uncomfortably. He wasn't a demonstrative man. "I'm so proud of you, honey."

"Thanks, Daddy!"

"Don't forget to turn the tassel to the other side when the president hands you your diploma."

"I won't forget."

THE CEREMONY WAS LONG, and the speaker was tedious. By the time he finished, the audience was restless, and Niki just wanted it over with.

She was third in line to get her diploma. She thanked the dean, whipped her tassel to the other side as she walked offstage and grinned to herself, imagining her father's pleased expression.

It took a long time for all the graduates to get through the line, but at last it was over, and Niki was outside with her father, congratulating classmates and working her way to the parking lot.

She noted that, when they were inside the car, her father was frowning.

"I turned my tassel," she reminded him.

He sighed. "Sorry, honey. I was thinking about Blair."

Her heart jumped. "Did you call Jameson?"

"Yes. He finally admitted that Blair hasn't been sober for three days. Apparently, the divorce is final, and Blair found out some unsavory things about his wife."

"Oh, dear." She tried not to feel pleasure that Blair was free. He'd said often enough that he thought of Niki as a child. "What sort of things?"

"I can't tell you, honey. It's very private stuff."

She drew in a long breath. "We should go get him and bring him to the ranch," she said firmly. "He shouldn't be on his own in that sort of mood."

He smiled softly. "You know, I was just thinking the same thing. Call Dave and have them get the Learjet over here. You can come with me if you like."

"Thanks."

He shrugged. "I might need the help," he mused. "Blair gets a little dangerous when he drinks, but he'd never hit a woman," he added.

She nodded. "Okay."

BLAIR DIDN'T RESPOND to her father's voice asking him to open the door. Muffled curses came through the wood, along with sounds of a big body bumping furniture.

"Let me try," Niki said softly. She rapped on the door. "Blair?" she called.

There was silence, followed by the sound of footsteps coming closer. "Niki?" came a deep, slurred voice.

"Yes, it's me."

He unlocked the door and opened it. He looked terrible. His face was flushed from too much alcohol. His black, wavy hair was ruffled. His blue shirt, unbuttoned and untucked, looking as if he'd slept in it. So did his black pants. He was a little unsteady on his feet. His eyes roved over Niki's face with warm affection.

She reached out and caught his big hand in both of hers. "You're coming home with us," she said gently. "Come on, now."

"Okay," he said, without a single protest.

Jameson, standing to one side, out of sight, sighed with relief. He grinned at her father.

Blair drew in a long breath. "I'm pretty drunk."

"That's okay," Niki said, still holding tight to his hand. "We won't let you drive."

He burst out laughing. "Damned little brat," he muttered.

She grinned at him.

"You dressed up to come visit me?" he asked, looking from her to her father.

"It was my graduation today," Niki said.

Blair grimaced. "Damn! I meant to come. I really did. I even got you a present." He patted his pockets. "Oh, hell, it's in my desk. Just a minute."

He managed to stagger over to the desk without falling. He dredged out a small wrapped gift. "But you can't open it until I'm sober," he said, putting it in her hands.

"Oh. Well, okay," she said. She cocked her head. "Are you planning to have to run me down when I open it, then?"

His eyes twinkled. "Who knows?"

"We'd better go before he changes his mind," her father said blithely.

"I won't," Blair promised. "There's too damned much available liquor here. You only keep cognac and Scotch whiskey," he reminded his friend.

"I've had Edna hide the bottles, though," her father assured him.

"I've had enough anyway."

"Yes, you have. Come on," Niki said, grabbing Blair's big hand in hers.

He followed her like a lamb, not even complaining at her assertiveness. He didn't notice that Todd and Jameson were both smiling with pure amusement.

WHEN THEY GOT back to Catelow, and the Ashton ranch, Niki led Blair up to the guest room and set him down on the big bed.

"Sleep," she said, "is the best thing for you."

He drew in a ragged breath. "I haven't slept for days," he confessed. "I'm so tired, Niki."

She smoothed back his thick, cool black hair. "You'll get past this," she said with a wisdom far beyond her years. "It only needs time. It's fresh, like a raw wound. You have to heal until it stops hurting so much."

He was enjoying her soft hand in his hair. Too much. He let out a long sigh. "Some days I feel my age."

"You think you're old?" she chided. "We've got a cowhand, Mike, who just turned seventy. Know what he did yesterday? He learned to ride a bicycle."

His eyebrows arched. "Are you making a point?"

"Yes. Age is only in the mind."

He smiled sardonically. "My mind is old, too."

"I'm sorry you couldn't have had children," she lied

and felt guilty that she was glad about it. "Sometimes they make a marriage work."

"Sometimes they end it," he retorted.

"Fifty-fifty chance."

"Elise would never have risked her figure to have a child," he said coldly. "She even said so." He grimaced. "We had a hell of a fight after the Christmas I spent here. It disgusted me that she'd go to some party with her friends and not even bother to call to see how I was. She actually said to me the money was nice. It was a pity I came with it."

"I'm so sorry," she said with genuine sympathy. "I can't imagine the sort of woman who'd marry a man for what he had. I couldn't do that, even if I was dirt-poor."

He looked up into soft, pretty gray eyes. "No," he agreed. "You're the sort who'd get down in the mud with your husband and do anything you had to do to help him. Rare, Niki. Like that hothouse orchid pin I gave you for Christmas."

She smiled. "I wear it all the time. It's so beautiful."

"Like you."

She made a face. "I'm not beautiful."

"What's inside you is," he replied, and he wasn't kidding.

She flushed a little. "Thanks."

He drew in a breath and shuddered. "Oh, God…" He shot out of the bed, heading toward the bathroom. He barely made it to the toilet in time. He lost his breakfast and about a fifth of bourbon.

When he finished, his stomach hurt. And there was Niki, with a wet washcloth. She bathed his face, helped him to the sink to wash out his mouth then helped him back to bed.

He couldn't help remembering his mother, his sweet

French mother, who'd sacrificed so much for him, who'd cared for him, loved him. It hurt him to remember her. He'd thought Elise resembled her. But it was this young woman, this angel, who was like her.

"Thanks," he managed to croak out.

"You'll be all right," she said. "But just in case, I'm going downstairs right now to hide all the liquor."

There was a lilt in her voice. He lifted the wet cloth he'd put over his eyes and peered up through a growing massive headache. She was smiling. It was like the sun coming out.

"Better hide it good," he teased.

She grinned. "Can I get you anything before I leave?"

"No, honey. I'll be fine."

Honey. Her whole body rippled as he said the word. She tried to hide her reaction to it, but she didn't have the experience for such subterfuge. He saw it and worried. He couldn't afford to let her get too attached to him. He was too old for her. Nothing would change that.

She got up, moving toward the door.

"Niki," he called softly.

She turned.

"Thanks," he said huskily.

She only smiled, before she went out and closed the door behind her.

Don't miss
WYOMING RUGGED by Diana Palmer,
available December 2015 wherever
Harlequin® HQN books and ebooks are sold.
www.Harlequin.com

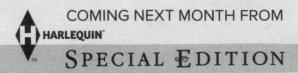
#2449 Fortune's Secret Heir
The Fortunes of Texas: All Fortune's Children
by Allison Leigh

The last thing Ella Thomas expects when she's hired to work a fancy party is to meet Prince Charming...yet that's what she finds in millionaire businessman Ben Robinson. But can the sexy tech mogul open up his heart to find his very own Cinderella?

#2450 Having the Cowboy's Baby
Brighton Valley Cowboys
by Judy Duarte

Country singer Carly Rayburn wants to focus on her promising singing career—so she reluctantly cuts off her affair with sexy cowboy Ian McAllister. But when she discovers she's pregnant with his child, she finds so much more in the arms of the rugged rancher.

#2451 The Widow's Bachelor Bargain
The Bachelors of Blackwater Lake
by Teresa Southwick

When real estate developer Sloan Holden meets beautiful widow Maggie Potter, he does his best to resist his attraction to the single mom. But a family might just be in store for this Blackwater Lake trio...one that only Sloan, Maggie and her daughter can build together!

#2452 Abby, Get Your Groom!
The Camdens of Colorado
by Victoria Pade

Dylan Camden hires Abby Crane to style his sister for her wedding...but his motives aren't pure. To make amends for the Camden clan's past wrongdoings, Dylan must make Abby aware of her past. But what's a bachelor to do when he falls for the very girl he's supposed to help?

#2453 Three Reasons to Wed
The Cedar River Cowboys
by Helen Lacey

Widower Grady Parker isn't looking to replace the wife he's loved and lost. Marissa Ellis is hardly looking for love herself—let alone with the handsome husband of her late best friend. But fate and Grady's three little girls have other ideas!

#2454 A Marine for His Mom
Sugar Falls, Idaho
by Christy Jeffries

When single mom Maxine Walker's young son launches a military pen pal project, she's just glad her child has a male role model in his life. But nobody expected Gunnery Sergeant Matthew Cooper to steal the hearts of everyone in the small town of Sugar Falls, Idaho—especially Maxine's!

YOU CAN FIND MORE INFORMATION ON UPCOMING HARLEQUIN® TITLES, FREE EXCERPTS AND MORE AT WWW.HARLEQUIN.COM.

HSECNM1215

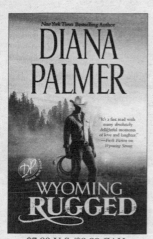

New York Times Bestselling Author

DIANA PALMER

"It's a fast read with many absolutely delightful moments of love and laughter."
—*Fresh Fiction* on *Wyoming Strong*

WYOMING RUGGED

$7.99 U.S./$9.99 CAN.

EXCLUSIVE
Limited time offer!

$1.00 OFF

New York Times bestselling author

DIANA PALMER

brings you back to Wyoming with a tale of love born in Big Sky Country…

WYOMING RUGGED

Available November 24, 2015.

Pick up your copy today!

HQN™

$1.00 OFF the purchase price of
WYOMING RUGGED by Diana Palmer.

Offer valid from November 24, 2015, to December 31, 2015.
Redeemable at participating retail outlets. Not redeemable at Barnes & Noble.
Limit one coupon per purchase. Valid in the U.S.A. and Canada only.

52613050

5 65373 00076 2   (8100)0 12096

Canadian Retailers: Harlequin Enterprises Limited will pay the face value of this coupon plus 10.25¢ if submitted by customer for this product only. Any other use constitutes fraud. Coupon is nonassignable. Void if taxed, prohibited or restricted by law. Consumer must pay any government taxes. Void if copied. Inmar Promotional Services ("IPS") customers submit coupons and proof of sales to Harlequin Enterprises Limited, P.O. Box 3000, Saint John, NB E2L 4L3, Canada. Non-IPS retailer—for reimbursement submit coupons and proof of sales directly to Harlequin Enterprises Limited, Retail Marketing Department, 225 Duncan Mill Rd., Don Mills, Ontario M3B 3K9, Canada.

U.S. Retailers: Harlequin Enterprises Limited will pay the face value of this coupon plus 8¢ if submitted by customer for this product only. Any other use constitutes fraud. Coupon is nonassignable. Void if taxed, prohibited or restricted by law. Consumer must pay any government taxes. Void if copied. For reimbursement submit coupons and proof of sales directly to Harlequin Enterprises Limited, P.O. Box 880478, El Paso, TX 88588-0478, U.S.A. Cash value 1/100 cents.

® and ™ are trademarks owned and used by the trademark owner and/or its licensee.

© 2015 Harlequin Enterprises Limited

PHDP1215COUPR

SPECIAL EXCERPT FROM

(H) HARLEQUIN®

SPECIAL EDITION

*When tycoon Ben Robinson enlists temp Ella Thomas
to help him uncover Fortune family secrets, will the
closed-off Prince Charming be able to resist the charms
of his beautiful Cinderella?*

Read on for a sneak preview of
FORTUNE'S SECRET HEIR, the first installment in the
2016 Fortunes of Texas twentieth anniversary continuity,
***ALL FORTUNE'S CHILDREN**.*

Ben figured it was only a matter of time before the security
guards came to check that he'd exited. But having gotten
what he'd come for, he had no reason to stay.

He went out the door and it closed automatically behind
him. When he tested it out of curiosity, it was locked.

"Crazy old bat," he muttered under his breath.

But he didn't really believe it.

Kate Fortune was many things. Of that he was certain.

But crazy wasn't one of them.

He looked around, getting his bearings before setting
off to his left. It was dark, only a few lights situated here
and there to show off some landscape feature. But he soon
made his way around the side of the enormous house and
to the front, which was not just well lit, but magnificently
so. He stopped at the valet and handed over his ticket to a
skinny kid in a black shirt and trousers.

He tried to imagine Ella dashing off the way this kid
was to retrieve his car, parked somewhere on the vast
property. He couldn't quite picture it.

But in his head, he could picture *her* quite clearly.

Not the red hair. That just reminded him of Stephanie. But the faint gap in her toothy smile and the clear light shining from her pretty eyes.

That was all Ella.

A moment later, when the valet returned with his Porsche, Ben got in and drove away.

Don't miss
FORTUNE'S SECRET HEIR
by New York Times *bestselling author Allison Leigh,*
available January 2016 wherever
Harlequin® Special Edition books and ebooks are sold.

www.Harlequin.com

HSEEXP1215

REQUEST YOUR FREE BOOKS!

2 FREE NOVELS PLUS 2 FREE GIFTS!

H HARLEQUIN®

SPECIAL EDITION

Life, Love & Family

HSE15

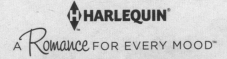